The Guest Bedroom

AJ Carter

Papyrus

Copyright © 2024 by Papyrus Publishing LTD.
All rights reserved. No part of this publication may be reproduced, distributed, or transmitted in any form or by any means, including photocopying, recording, or other electronic or mechanical methods, without the prior written permission of the publisher, except in the case of brief quotations embodied in critical reviews and certain other non-commercial uses permitted by copyright law. For permission requests, write to the publisher, addressed "Attention: Permissions Coordinator," at the address below.

contact@ajcarterbooks.com

Dedication

For my daughter, who inspires everything I do.

And for my dog, who farts in her sleep.

The Guest Bedroom

Chapter 1
Becca

THIS IS the life of a stay-at-home mother.

It begins with waking up at an ungodly hour to torturous screaming. You shoot from your half-doze and rush to the baby's bedroom, sort of knowing what to expect and yet somehow still thinking something might have gone horribly wrong. I mean, the screaming is like nothing you've ever heard before, and the protector in you can't help but wonder...

Then comes the best part of your day – the eyes of your six-month-old lighting up as you enter the room. You speak like you've sucked on a helium balloon pump. The baby's smile widens, the eyes glistening with innocent joy. It makes the coming nappy change a lot easier.

As soon as you're done cleaning what can only be described as a 'poonami', it's time to get the food going. At six months, you're starting to introduce solid foods, which means preparing a sickening variety of tasters that will inevitably end up on the floor. All the while, you know it's only a matter of time before that precious little bundle of joy starts wailing, so you have a very finite window in which to wash the dishes and – if you're lucky – brush your teeth over the kitchen sink so as not to miss your child potentially choking.

That's just the first hour of parenting each morning.

And I love every last second of it.

My husband's day is somewhat different. We've had so many conversations about how hard it is to leave his family at home while he goes out to earn some money. It seems the grass is always greener; I would love the break, and there's nothing Jordan wants more than to spend some quality time with our only child. One day we might meet in the middle, but until then...

Today is just like any other. I've taken Jax to one of the only two baby groups in our small, peaceful little town. After spending an hour and a half mingling with the other mothers (who all do

The Guest Bedroom

nothing but whine about how little their husbands are doing), it's time to do some shopping. Jax loves sitting in the trolley, pointing at every single thing that has even the faintest touch of colour. It's hard to describe how much I love my child, but I'll try.

I would die for him.

Not that I'll ever have to. The boy's father is a police officer, and we live far from any kind of threat. Our life is one of those film-like fantasies; we have a large house that we inherited when Jordan's parents died in a storm while hiking, enough money to live on comfortably if at least one of us works, and we're all insanely healthy. Some might say we have the perfect lives, which is a stretch but probably true. Although it does make me think…

Something must eventually go wrong.

I just didn't think that would be today.

It happens when Jordan comes home from work. I'm in the kitchen, using two boiled carrots I've cut into shapes to entertain Jax in his high chair. A high-pitched giggle shrieks from his mouth, happy tears coming to my eyes. God, that laugh is like cocaine. I love it (the laugh, not cocaine – my husband is a police officer, I'll have you know).

Jordan comes in and dumps a work bag on the dining chair, then comes and kisses me on the cheek. I lean back and let him at it, allowing Jax to see how lovers should interact with each other on a daily basis. Jordan's stubble tickles me as usual, and I shiver giddily.

'How's my little man?' he asks, leaning over to say hi to his son, whose mouth is open wide in a gasp of sheer delight. 'Did you do lots of little poopies, buddy? *Did you do lots of teeny-tiny poopies in your little poo-poo pants?*'

Jax giggles hysterically, which instantly brings a smile to my face. It's always like this – within seconds of my husband coming in the door, all three of us are having a laughing fit. It's one of the many, many moments I wish we could keep forever.

As time goes by, Jordan tries turning his back to make a round of drinks. I entertain Jax with more shaped foods to occupy him for a moment. Meanwhile, the kettle bubbles and boils behind me, the clanging of cutlery against china dinging like a bell. A few seconds later, the amazing smell of coffee fills the air, giving me what my friend used to call a 'smellgasm'.

'I bumped into your friend today,' Jordan says,

The Guest Bedroom

putting a cup behind me on the dining table. I nod to thank him, but he continues telling me about this mysterious friend of mine. 'She was asking about you. Wanted to know where you live.'

'Oh?' I'm still making faces at Jax. 'Who was it?'

'Honestly, I don't recall her name.'

'Would you know it if I said it?'

'Probably. Began with M.'

Maybe it's the fact that I know a lot of people – or it could be that I'm running on four hours of poor-quality sleep and my brain feels like it's been tenderised by The Incredible Hulk – but I can't think of a single friend whose name starts with M.

'That has to be wrong,' I tell him.

'No, it was definitely an M.'

'Can you describe her?'

'Around five-ten, jet-black hair, bone-thin with beady little eyes. Actually, at first I thought she was homeless. I was five seconds away from giving her some change, but then she mentioned something about how you went to school together.'

It's killing me. I moved away from my home town fifteen years ago and never looked back. Even then, I didn't have many friends. There was one girl who died (call me crazy, but I highly suspect she isn't the one asking about me), and one other person who I hoped to never hear from again, or I just might lose my mind even more than she did.

It dawns over me like a cloud. The memory slingshots back into my mind, my heart thumping as the events replay themselves. I shake them off, doing my best to ignore them and praying that I'm wrong. I must be, because it should be impossible for her to have followed me here. That's the control that woman has over me – instant paralysis at the mere mention of her name. Which is exactly what I get when Jordan snaps his fingers.

'That's it,' he says like it means nothing. 'Her name was Megan.'

But it's not *nothing*.

It's everything I ever feared.

Have you ever felt so horrified by the mere mention of someone's name?

That's what happens to me with Megan List.

It's on the tip of my tongue like a poison, even hours after Jordan came home. As usual, when he's done spending time with Jax and putting him to bed, he fell asleep in front of the TV. I should be using this time to catch up on some chores or even

The Guest Bedroom

a little sleep, but all I can think about is that blast from the past. It's clogging up my every thought, as you can imagine when one's perfectly crafted, peaceful home life has been violated.

Yes, her name alone did that to me.

I open up my laptop, my fingers tense on my trembling hands. My sight travels to Jordan, who doesn't move even after I've typed Megan's name into every social media site. No matter how hard I look, there's not a single mention of her anywhere. It's like she's become a ghost, without a single footprint in the entire digital world. If I'd done half the things she had, I wouldn't be putting myself on public display either. She might as well be wearing a sign that says, 'Yoo-hoo, Mr. Policeman! Come and get me!'

Not that the police can do much about it either.

A past like hers needs to be proved.

Sighing, I close my laptop. The soft clap makes Jordan stir. I watch him with admiration, cherishing him with every last ounce of my love. That man is my hero – my best friend. I always wondered what it would be like if he knew the truth about me. It would destroy him, his misguided belief that he'd met the perfect woman beaten like Apollo Creed by that Russian. The years we've spent together would melt away, my future confined to a prison cell.

The thought alone plagues me. Women like me never fare well in prison. The best I could hope for is that the other inmates hear the reason for my conviction and don't make me trade sexual favours for extra jelly pots. Not that my fear wouldn't give me away – a simple croak in my voice would betray me, and before I know it my neck would be plastered in love bites. It's enough to make me feel sick, and to know that no matter what happens, Jordan can never, *ever* find out what I did all those years ago.

There's only one person who knows that secret.

Her name is Megan, and she's looking for me.

SOMEHOW, I manage to put her out of my mind for the rest of the night. I sleep well, dream even easier, then wake up to a screaming baby all over again. You know the routine by now, so I set to doing all of that and waking up the house. It's like clockwork at this point, my body taking care of business while my brain is still fast asleep.

The Guest Bedroom

Just like every other day, Jordan kisses me goodbye, then Jax and I start our creative play. We're building blocks and finger-painting today – we should be going out for a walk, but I'm nervous about bumping into Megan. What if she sees me and decides to latch on? Why is she even in town? The place we grew up in is so far from here and, honestly, there's nothing worth seeing in Collingwood. Basically, there's no way in hell she came here without wanting something in particular, and the fact she was asking around for me...

It's well into the afternoon when I see her. There I was, minding my own business and on damage control, picking up discarded toys while Jax crawls around to play with the others, when a gliding silhouette outside the window catches my eye. The doorbell rings then, and I freeze on the spot, still processing what I just saw.

Who I just saw.

For a minute, I think it's my mind playing tricks on me, but then the doorbell rings again. Jax almost falls over as he turns in his crawling position to look up at me, his face a twisted expression of confusion. Now that I think about it, he hasn't heard the doorbell before – we never have visitors, and we're rarely home when the postman comes.

So then, who I saw passing the window must be real.

Apprehensive, I go to the window and press my cheek to the glass. It's hard to see the front doorstep from here, but I try my best. All I can see is the sleeve of someone's jacket – a dusty-brown thing that looks like it's been through too many washes. It's not something I ever imagined Megan wearing – she always favoured plain, black clothing that hugged her skinny frame – and yet I know it's her just from the posture in her shadow that reaches across the lawn.

Then she turns.

It's childish, but I duck beneath the window. I've forgotten to breathe, and Jax excitedly crawls towards me as if it's some kind of game. All the while, there's a rap upon the glass above us, and I peer to see that ghost from years ago staring right down at me. No, it's not a game – this could be the reckoning I've been waiting for all these years.

And it's time to pay the piper.

Chapter 2
Becca

I FEEL LIKE AN IDIOT.

Here I am, squatting under the window to hide from a woman who's already seen me. Jax is giggling in my arms like it's hilarious. If he only knew how serious this is, the laughter would end and the tears would begin. Tears, just like the ones that kept me up at night for so many years. The same kind of tears that made me relocate and start a new life.

'I can see you, Becca,' a muffled voice comes through the window. 'Open up.'

It's dumb, I know, but I clamber off the floor and act as if this was the first time I've seen her. A big, stupid grin creeps on to my face as I wave a hand, scoop Jax up into my arms, and head towards the front door. My mouth is already dry, nervousness making my tongue feel like sandpaper as I move to greet the ghost from all those years ago.

As soon as the door opens, Megan tilts her head with a mocking grin. She hasn't changed; her eyes are still hollows set behind gaunt, pale cheeks. Her black hair is straight and neat, but she probably wouldn't care if the wind messed it up. She's gripping a backpack by the hanging strap, and her stick-thin figure is garbed in tight, black clothes with a brown jacket over the top. Even her dress sense is exactly the same as before.

'Were you hiding from me?' she asks.

'Of course not. How are you, Megan?'

'I'm okay.' Her eyes drift to Jax, who's squirming like a worm in my arms. Then her eyes light up, which I find nothing short of alarming. A smile bursts out as she leans in. 'Wow, who is this little ray of sunshine?'

'This is my son, Jax.'

'Aw, he's beautiful. How old?'

'He's six months. Why are you here?'

Megan reels back and double-blinks, exaggerating the motion as if to act hurt. The smile, however, refuses to leave. 'I just wanted to catch up

The Guest Bedroom

with an old friend. I must admit, I expected a much warmer welcome than this.'

Yeah, I bet you did, I think while grinding my teeth.

See, here's the thing about Megan. She's a full-blown textbook narcissist. Not only will she ruin your life and seize every advantage along the way but, when the damage is done and the dust settles, she'll look back and ask what happened. If you expect her to take accountability for her actions, you can keep dreaming. It's the entitlement and lack of responsibility that makes her genuinely wonder why she wouldn't be welcome here.

I'm just about to think of something to say, but the chance doesn't come. Megan steps forward, tactfully talking as she invades my home. This is something she told me about years ago – talk while doing something the other person won't like. They'll be so distracted by what you're saying that they can't find time to tell you no. I hate that it works, even though I know the trick and badly want to say something.

'It's a lovely place you have here,' she tells me, stepping into the hallway and gazing around at the crystal chandelier, the open lobby, and the long hallways that split in either direction. 'Looks fit for a queen, but I always thought of you more as a princess.'

'Goes to show how much you know me,' I bite.

'Meow,' she mocks. 'Why so bitter?'

'You know we don't have the best past.'

'Surely, there's a reason to change that.'

'Is there? My life is a good one. I'm happy.'

'And I'm very happy to hear that.' Megan turns to look me dead in the eye. Finally, her smile dies. She comes towards me, slowly with her head down, then meets my gaze again. 'Look, things didn't end in the best way, did they? I understand that, and I've grown up. What I'd like to do is right some wrongs, repair broken friendships, and set myself on the right track. It might not look great, but that's the truth. Can we try again, Becca?'

I must admit, it's coming across pretty sincerely. Not that I'm dumb enough to let my guard down, but Jax is still squirming, his tiny little knees digging into my stomach as he tries to get away. All the while, Megan is staring at me and hoping for approval. The worst thing is, I want to give it to her but only for my own selfish needs. If I can stay in her good books, my secret might stay safe. Then again, if I upset her...

We're both distracted by the car pulling up

outside. Jax knows what this means, and he starts to writhe even harder as his baby-blue eyes light up. He excitedly points over my shoulder and laughs, but he's not the only one excited to see Jordan arrive.

Megan also has her sights on him.

'Oh, is this your husband?' she asks as she passes. 'I'd love to see him again.'

I turn on the spot and try to tell her no, but I'm trying to catch Jax as he escapes my death grip. By now, Megan is already outside and introducing herself to Jordan. I'm dying to catch his eye and give him the signal that she's not welcome here, but by then she's already invited to stay for dinner. Just like that, Megan is in my life again.

Just like that, I'm miserable.

THE AFTERNOON IS FILLED with empty conversation about the weather and the state of the town. Megan takes an interest in Jordan's work – he's a police officer, which is often a topic of conversation – but she visibly shrinks away when he jokes about arresting her.

That's because she knows what she's done.

We both do.

It's getting too late to start cooking, so we order Chinese food and go nuts. Megan offers to dip her hand in her pocket, but Jordan insists we cover it. We're doing well financially speaking, but I don't like the idea that we're paying for this woman to eat after everything she's done to me. Not that he's aware of her sins, but I am. That's why it hurts.

By the time we make it past all the small talk, we're sitting around the dining table with seventy pounds worth of food between us all. We have full plates, which are as slick with grease as the air is of hot deliciousness. I'm not eating much – my stomach is quite unsettled while my greatest enemy is sitting across the table – so I focus on keeping Jax fed on soft samplings and some of his own vegetables I prepared earlier.

As I spoon that into his eager mouth, I'm starting to question whether Megan might have been genuine in her claims to start a new life. What was it she said? Righting wrongs? So far, I've not seen even the slightest indication that she intends to let out my secret. But that doesn't keep my nerves at bay. I could lose everything in a heartbeat if she does.

'So,' Jordan says, dabbing his mouth with a napkin. 'How exactly do you know Becca?'

Megan and I exchange a glance. Nothing is said between us. Not with words, anyway. I shoot her a look as if to plead for her silence. To my surprise, she ignores me completely and goes straight in, proving that she really is here for peace.

'We went to school together,' she says. 'We were great friends.'

'Oh? Don't take this the wrong way, but I've never heard of you.'

'It's because you don't listen,' I counter jokingly.

We all laugh, but Megan does a poor job at hiding she's upset. She entertains herself by pushing chow mein around her plate with a fork. Meanwhile, I'm holding my breath and praying he doesn't ask the wrong questions. The ones that will land me in trouble.

'Have you ladies not caught up in a while?' he asks.

'We lost touch actually,' Megan explains.

'How did you find her in the end?'

'Social media.'

Now, I know that's a lie. Megan doesn't have social media – I checked. So this can only mean one thing... she's been keeping tabs on me all these years. It wouldn't surprise me, either.

Obsession and controlling behaviour are kind of her thing. At least when aggression has left the room, but I try not to remind myself of that side of her.

'And what brings you here now?' Jordan presses.

'Such a cop,' I say with a fake chortle. 'What's with the interrogation?'

'I'm just trying to learn about our guest.'

'It's fine.' Megan smiles and sets down her fork. 'To be completely honest, I came here because I need help. Collingwood is somewhere I've always wanted to live, so it was worth me visiting. When I found out Becca lives here, I rushed at the chance to stop by and see my old school friend. Only problem is, I was dumb enough not to book a hotel and now they're all fully booked. I feel so stupid, but...'

She leaves it right there, perfectly comfortable in the silence she created. It's purposeful, just like everything she does. She knows for a fact that Jordan will fall for her pity party, and that I can't do a thing to stop it because, let's face it, she has power over me. So I wait there in the elongated pause, hoping beyond hope that Jordan doesn't say what I think he will.

The Guest Bedroom

Then, as if to put the cherry on this ugly-as-hell cake, he makes the offer.

'You're welcome to stay here,' he says. 'If that's okay with Becca?'

All eyes on the table turn to look at me.

As if I have any choice.

WE SET Megan up in the guest bedroom, and she retires there early without much more than a simple 'good night'. The hours on the road are her excuse, and that's fine. It gives me a chance to speak to Jordan about what the hell just happened.

It comes as a surprise to him. Apparently, he was completely under the illusion that I really liked Megan and that having her here might be nice. If anything, that just goes to show how well I hid my anxiety about being in her presence. It feels wrong, you know – sitting around and waiting for her to unleash the truth, bringing the walls of my life crashing down around me. Maybe I'm wrong though, and she really is trying to fix things.

Then again, maybe she's just as manipulative as ever.

'Do you want me to ask her to leave?' Jordan asks, peeling back the duvet and patting down his pillows as per routine. I help him fold back the quilt, but he holds my eye. 'It wouldn't be a problem, you know. I don't want you to be uncomfortable in your own home.'

'I'm not uncomfortable,' I blurt too snappishly. 'Well, a little, but...'

We crawl into bed. I lay in my husband's arms, feeling safer than I have all day, but it will never be enough. Not while I'm aware of the monster staying in the guest bedroom. I keep an eye on the baby monitor, where Jax stirs in a black-and-white room with fuzzy ambience from the white noise machine. *I'm* safe, sure, but is *he?*

I think back to how she looked at him. It sent a shiver right through me, and the discomfort still hasn't left. Jordan brushes my hair with his big hands, then kisses me on the head. It's his way of saying goodnight without actually saying it, because he wants me to know that he'll be here all night if I need him. Which I will, because this is the most scared I've been in a long time. Megan is quite convincing in telling me how she wants to start fresh, but am I stupid to believe her or am I just being paranoid? Time will tell.

Until then, I'll keep a close eye on her.

Chapter 3
Jordan

Don't get me wrong, I love my wife.

But I saw the way Megan looked at me.

Just to be incredibly clear, I have never and will never cheat. It's just not in me. However, there is this small, dark corner of my mind that often wonders what it might be like if I did. It's nothing more than a fantasy really, which is apparently very normal. A fantasy I'll never forget, because I have a sneaking suspicion it will keep me occupied in my more private moments.

Now, I want to put some more emphasis on how much I love Becca. She's been my best friend for years, and we've been married for most of those. Do we have our own little squabbles about petty things? Of course we do, especially since Jax was born. But something we've always been extremely efficient at is communication. If there's a problem, we'll make some hot chocolate and talk it out until we find a happy middle ground. It still winds her up when I leave my socks lying around, and it still aggravates me when she cuts me off mid-sentence, but all in all we stay on top of our problems.

With that out of the way, I want to talk about the second time I saw Megan.

It was quiet at work, so I managed to clock out a couple of hours early and head home. There was a raven-haired beauty waiting to welcome me when I arrived. The first time I met her, I'd given her our home address on the condition she didn't tell Becca, and it felt like we'd bonded over that secret. Now she was here to greet me, an eerily excitable smile somehow creating dimples in her gaunt cheeks. I got out of the car, mildly aware that Becca was watching from the front door, and did my best to act shocked at the very sight of her. It played out well, I think, and eventually led to me inviting Megan to dinner.

Mostly just so I could see her for even longer.

Becca protested, which surprised me and made

me curious at the same time. Why was she so concerned about this woman staying with us? Perhaps she'd picked up on the same vibes I had, and also thought Megan might have secretly wanted me. I hope that's true, because it lends a little credibility to the idea that I am actually an attractive man. A *desired* man.

Then there was the other thing. After the food and the talking at the dinner table, there was a bit of coming and going between Becca and myself as we prepared Jax for his bath and bedtime. It was a rocky hour, but we crushed it with our typical level of teamwork. I was thinking of Megan the whole time – again, just a fantasy – and this whole little mental sexual adventure only got better as the night went on. Because it didn't end at a nice dinner and an invitation to stay for as long as she needed to. I offered Megan the guest bedroom and, as she made her way towards it to disappear for the night, she turned just long enough to smile.

Then shot me a wink.

As IF ALL of that wasn't enough, Becca had to go and throw a spanner in the works by acting the way she was. We were just getting into bed when she started to show some reluctance to having Megan stay with us. That's the problem with being a cop – you quickly discover when someone is acting differently than usual and, nine times out of ten, it's because they're hiding something.

So, what is my wife hiding?

Over dinner I started to notice she would go quiet whenever the subject of their past came up. Neither of them said anything to suggest there had been trouble, but sometimes actions speak louder than words. Even a blind man could have seen the way they glanced at each other across the table. There was something unspoken. Something bad.

And Becca was terrified it would come out.

To be one hundred per cent truthful with you, I don't really care that much. It could be something so trivial, like Becca trying out a girl-on-girl relationship that she's too embarrassed to talk about. It could be a falling out over a boy that got out of hand. If Becca wants to tell me, she's more than welcome to do so when she's feeling comfortable enough. I never was one to prod and poke and mess around with people's emotions.

Still, it was intriguing.

Come bedtime, it got even worse. Becca

The Guest Bedroom

expressed a deep displeasure in having that woman under our roof. I did all the things a good husband and father should do – making sure we're safe, that there's nothing threatening about our mysterious new guest – but it was like getting blood out of a stone. That only supported my theory Becca was hiding something.

She falls asleep pretty quickly after that brief discussion, but I stay up for a while wondering what Megan was up to. I plan to check her convictions at the office tomorrow morning, but for now I want to just imagine heading into the guest bedroom and letting her know her wink was well received. What would I even say to her? I guess something along the lines of making sure she's comfortable and that we're just down the hall if she needs anything. A thin veil for 'I want to have sex with you'.

But again, I have to make sure this stays in my imagination. Whatever *could* happen between us is nothing more than hypothetical. I love my wife – I've said it a thousand times and will say it a thousand more – but a man can wonder... can't he?

It reaches three in the morning, and I give up on sleeping. I turn to my book for support, then find myself staring at the same page for minutes on end. My mind is buzzing. I'm too distracted. All I can think about is that wink, and how the woman I married has a secret past she's not willing to share with me. The truth will come out in time, I suppose.

Until then, I'll just have fun with my thoughts.

Chapter 4
Becca

JORDAN IS ONLY WORKING a half-day today (thank God), but that still leaves me alone in the house with Megan. Thankfully, she doesn't so much as stir until after he's left for work, so at least I get a chance to get through Jax's morning routine and think of what I'll say to her.

It's a hard thing, reconnecting with someone you really wished you'd never see again. There's a fine line to tread, balancing somewhere between casual chit-chat and the occasional link to our past. Even if she does want to improve herself, Megan has a long way to go. It will also involve exercising a little trust from my end. Which I'm probably not capable of.

I'm making pancakes when Megan first

surfaces from the guest bedroom, rubbing her eyes as she scuffs her feet along the tiled kitchen floor. I offer a lazy smile then fan the steam out of my face before flipping the half-made pancake.

'That smells nice,' she says, peering over my shoulder with rancid morning breath.

'They're for Jax, but I could rustle some up for you, too?'

'Nah, I never really liked eating breakfast. Makes me feel sick.'

Breakfast, lunch, dinner. Megan always was scarily thin, her ribcage easily discernible even through her T-shirts. She's a little heavier these days but not much.

She pulls out a chair and seats herself at the dining table, where Jax is focusing hard on eating the sliced banana I left as a distraction. I'm watching over my shoulder while I cook, not wanting to take my eye off her for so much as a second. I know what she's capable of.

'What have you got planned for the day?' I ask, mostly to kill the awkward silence.

'Not a lot. I was thinking of exploring the town a little.'

'There isn't a ton to do in Collingwood.'

'Which is ideal for me. I'm sick of the chaos.'

The Guest Bedroom

'Mmhmm.'

I scoop out the pancakes and leave them to cool on Jax's little rubber plate, with every intention of tearing them apart shortly. Until then, I turn and fold my arms, leaning back against the kitchen counter while Megan leans in to play with my son.

'Please don't,' I say. 'He gets too easily distracted.'

'What, so I can't play with him?' Megan pouts.

'Not right now. He needs to eat in a minute.'

With a sigh, she sits back and rakes her fingers through her messy black hair. It falls down her back when she lets go and starts gazing around the room. She reminds me of a bored teenager, desperately searching for something to do.

Then she finds my eyes.

'I always wanted kids,' she says. 'You're lucky.'

'You never found the right person?'

'Not exactly.'

That's a good thing. Trust me. Megan is the worst person I've ever met, and that extends to every inch of her personality. There's nobody less fitting to be a mother than that woman. Even if she does appear okay on the surface. Even if she does seem sane.

'Well,' Megan stands and stretches. 'Maybe

someday, hey?'

'Yeah, maybe.'

As she heads for the same door she so recently came in through, she stops long enough to stare back at Jax. A cold spike drives into the back of my neck, making me shiver. It's something in her eyes that does it, or maybe just the *absence* of something. A certain humanity that I've never known to exist within her. It only makes it more disturbing that she's watching my son. Especially when those last words linger in the air like an odour.

'Maybe someday,' she said.

My shivers are justified.

I BARELY SEE her for the rest of the day, but she does make a show of banging and crashing around. Even with something as simple as leaving her room to use the toilet, she's slamming the seat down and whacking the utility doors shut while she rummages through for something. Feminine products, possibly, or just some dental floss. Who cares?

She doesn't make her next appearance until Jordan pulls up on the drive. The sound of crunching gravel echoes through the house. Jax suddenly forgets about his cuddly pig toy as excitement courses through him. He gasps excitedly, incredibly eager to crawl towards the front door. He's still finding the concept hard to grasp, but it's amazing that he's trying. With determination like that, he'll go far in life.

By the time we get to the front door, Megan is already there. The door is wide open, and she doesn't so much as look at me when I ask her to move aside. Instead, she waits while Jordan comes up the drive and asks where his family is. She ignores him, too.

'In here,' I call, peeved by her brattish behaviour.

Jordan comes in, addresses Megan with just the right level of attention, then turns all his energy towards Jax. Kissing me seems to come as an afterthought, but I'm okay with it. Our son needs more attention than I ever did and, besides, we both know we love each other.

Megan comes and goes over the next few minutes, as if she's not at all interested in being there. It's a far departure from the version of her we saw only yesterday, but whatever. I'm not interested in hosting or entertaining her. If anything, it's better she gets bored – it increases the chances of her packing up and letting me get on with my life.

The problem is, she suddenly takes an interest when we begin to make plans. Jordan has offered to take us out for coffee and cake. It's one of our favourite activities, because the café has a small sensory play area for Jax, and I get a chance to be outside of these walls with somebody other than the local mums. I'm practically salivating at the thought of that red velvet cake and caramel latte, but my good mood is killed when Megan returns.

'Where are we going?' she asks.

'Out for coffee,' I tell her, limiting how much she knows.

'Great! I love coffee. Let me get my jacket.'

Before anyone can protest, she's gone back to her bedroom. We don't have long to communicate this, but I pull a face at Jordan to let him know I don't want this. Without so much as a spoken word, I know he's apologetic but thinks it's rude to tell Megan no. Which means this afternoon isn't going to be anywhere near relaxing.

ALTHOUGH THE SEATING area is small, the rest of the café is huge, with a kids' play zone and a long slide that protrudes from a plastic tree. Jax isn't really old enough to know what all this stuff is, but

The Guest Bedroom

there's a familiarity that makes his head turn. There are other kids here today – just three of them – which might make him feel a bit more comfortable. But we'll worry about that in a while, when we've got our drinks and settled down.

It's Jordan who orders them, already knowing what I want but then asking Megan if she would like anything. Naturally, she grins and perks up as if she's just been invited to the school prom by her crush. I don't like it, and I stare at her long enough to let her know. Not that she notices I'm even looking in her direction.

Her attention is fixed on Jordan.

Well, I'm not about to compete for my own husband, so I take Jax and find one of the larger tables, setting up a high chair beside it. Thankfully, Jordan quickly pays up and comes over to help, first flattening the high chair food tray, then taking Jax from his sling and lowering him in. It's no surprise to see that Megan is following him around like a fly on a cow's arse, but there you go. It's starting to look like he's the reason she's here.

We sit around the table and make a fuss over Jax, then our coffee and cake is delivered by a moody young waitress who I think is the daughter of my secondary school bully. I thank her regardless and start picking at the red velvet, tasting the buttery cream on the tip of my tongue. I'm about to have one of those 'foodgasms' again.

'Slow down,' Megan says. 'A moment on the lips, a lifetime on the hips.'

I gawk at her, unamused. 'That's my own decision to make.'

'It's just a piece of advice, that's all.'

'Sadly for you, I don't want your advice. I'll eat what I like.'

'Okay, well, if you're sure you're comfortable with that...'

Megan gives that smug, pleased-with-herself smirk again, then carries on as if she didn't just come out with something offensive. I look to Jordan, whose eyes are wide open with disbelief, but he doesn't rush to my defence. Either he doesn't need to, or he doesn't want to.

'Why don't you tell us about your plans?' he says instead, addressing Megan.

Megan's smile drops. 'What plans?'

'For instance, where are you going to live? Where are you going to work?'

'Oh, I see. I'm not really qualified in anything.'

'That shouldn't be a problem. There's plenty of shop work, pubs, cafés, kitchens, and things to work in around here. If you plan on staying, that is.'

'I definitely do,' she says flirtatiously, which I don't like one bit.

'So, you're thirty-five years old,' he goes on, 'and you don't feel qualified in anything. What have you been doing all this time?'

'Just the odd thing here or there.'

'How very cryptic.'

'Intentionally.'

I roll my eyes and unscrew the lid of a yoghurt pouch for Jax, carefully placing it in his hands so he doesn't squirt it all over the place. Meanwhile, I feel Megan's eyes all over me. It's awful – it feels like a thousand bugs scurrying all over my skin. Goosebumps prickle the flesh, but she can't win. She *won't* intimidate me.

'Maybe there's a job back home for you,' I say, hinting for her to leave.

'Somehow, I don't think that's the best thing for me.'

'Why's that?'

'Mmm, too much history.'

'Ignore it. Make a new future.'

'No, thank you.'

Inside, I'm laughing. The tension is so thick

that even Jax has stopped sucking the pouch. Jordan is looking back and forth between us, like he knows there's something more going on. The fact he could find out the truth any minute now makes me sick, but I won't be bullied.

'Actually.' Megan takes a deep breath and looks down in her lap. 'You know what? Maybe you're right. I should start looking at my own past a little more. There's probably some deep-rooted trauma that makes me feel like I don't belong. I wonder what that might be...?'

Now my heart is racing. Jordan's gaze lands on me, and I don't know what to say. It's not so visible to the untrained eye, but Megan just threatened me. It's obvious in the way she punctuates 'past' and 'trauma' like it's not even herself she's talking about.

And she's not.

'Okay,' I tell her, hoping to calm her down. 'That's enough. Let's enjoy the cake.'

'Should we?' Megan says. 'Or should we tell Jordan a little something about you?'

Jordan sits up straight, crooking his head to one side. 'What's going on?'

'Nothing much. Just that your wife has been lying to you.'

The Guest Bedroom

'Don't,' I snap, but the word comes out in an empty, silent breath.

'Why don't you tell him, Becca?' she goes on. 'If you don't, I will.'

'Becca?' Jordan asks. 'Please explain.'

Every eye at the table is on me, each face holding different expressions; Jax is baffled, Jordan is confused, and Megan is grinning like some demon who's just found a new host to possess. My appetite is suddenly gone, so I shove the plate away and try to steady myself as anxiety sears through my body. My hands shake, so I hide them under the table.

'Becca?' Jordan prompts.

'Okay, I'll tell him,' Megan says, turning towards him.

I want to reach across the table and grab her, but who knows if she's bluffing? It would only make me look more guilty anyway, so all I can do is sit still and try to set a good example for Jax, hoping my marriage isn't about to come to an end.

'The truth is,' she says, 'Becca and I haven't been friends for a very long time.'

'Right...' Jordan says with hesitance. 'Why's that?'

'Because something serious happened a few

years ago.' She looks at me with menace, then looks back at my husband. 'We were besties for years, but there was someone who came between us. A woman, and... I don't know, I guess it stirred something in Becca's brain. She became jealous and finally understood that she might be a little bi-curious.'

Jordan smiles like he *wants* to believe it but doesn't. 'Seriously?'

'One hundred per cent. Becca?'

Megan looks at me with a devilish grin. What she just said is complete nonsense, but it's better than knowing what really happened all those years ago. Jordan's waiting to hear if any of that really happened and, just because I could undo it later, I don't hesitate to admit it.

'It's true,' I say. 'But it was just a phase.'

My husband nods, that smile riding on his lips a while longer as he continues eating his cake. Jax starts making funny, excitable noises, and Jordan then rushes to whip him out of the high chair and take him over to the play zone. Which just leaves me and Megan.

She doesn't say a word – just smiles to let me know my place.

That she's the one in control.

Chapter 5
Becca

A WHOLE DAY comes and goes, during which Megan seems completely... well, normal.

There are no snide remarks or cocky comments, no threats to tell my husband something he absolutely should not learn about me. In fact, she's super nice, offering to cook and clean and earn her keep. Jordan tells her not to, of course, ever the gentleman. But what he fails to realise is that whatever Megan doesn't have to clean, I do.

I love my husband – he works really hard and is a wonderful father – but sometimes I wish he wouldn't take me for granted. Tonight, for instance, I'm the one bathing Jax because Jordan has his face buried in a book. He's started reading for leisure since lockdown, and I'm so glad he's found himself a hobby, but I sort of wish he weren't so addicted to those books. They're crime novels, of course, so he jokes that they're for a work study and dodges the issue. Not just the issue that I need help, but that I'm always doing so much alone.

Anyway, I try to let it go and enjoy bath time. It's one of my favourite times of day, because Jax is all smiles and giggles. Even when I pour a cup of water over his little bald head to wash away the shampoo, he gazes up at me lovingly. I hope he knows how much his mother loves him. I know he loves me, too. It certainly feels that way.

I'm just wiping a baton of bubbles off my nose when Jax's laughing simmers into a cute gargling noise, then he splashes the water when he spots his favourite duck. I want to pick him up and cuddle him, but there will be time for that later, when I read to him before putting him down for sleep. My little man is my best friend, but don't tell Jordan that.

Speaking of, I can hear him outside the bathroom. Sometimes he likes to sneak up on me just to attack me with affectionate kisses. This time, though, I'm ready for him. There's a shadow of feet under the bathroom door, and the floorboards

The Guest Bedroom

groan under his weight. I stay there on my knees, playfully putting my finger to my lips just to include Jax in the game. Then, in the silence, we wait for Jordan to burst in.

Then we wait some more.

And some more...

It seems strange. He's usually done his thing by now, so there's a little cause for concern. However, I try not to let my imagination play tricks on me, simply making sure Jax is seated upright before reaching for the door handle. I move swiftly so as not to leave him unattended, yanking down the handle and ripping open the door. My mouth opens as I plan to jokingly announce that he's messed up – caught in the act.

But he's not there.

The floorboards creak again. I poke my head out the door. I half-expect to see Jordan running a mile, but the person I see is not my husband at all. Clear as day, I spot Megan shuffling down the hallway without looking back. She vanishes from sight a couple of seconds later, and I can't even pursue her because I'm watching Jax. There's no telling exactly why Megan was even upstairs, much less standing outside the bathroom.

But I do know it makes me feel uneasy.

. . .

It's amazing what being protective over your child can do.

For example, take the way Megan looked at Jax when she said she wanted kids someday. That was enough to stir panic in even the calmest of people, which some people might consider me to be. I felt immediate worry, too, but it's a bit like getting hit by lightning or winning the lottery – you hear about these things but never really think they'll happen to you.

Megan's little head game at the café also rubbed me up the wrong way, but where I draw the line is creeping around in the upstairs of our home. The guest bedroom, where she's staying for hopefully a small amount of time, is downstairs and connected to the living room. There's also a bathroom downstairs with a shower in it, so she has absolutely no reason to be going anywhere near the stairs unless there's some kind of emergency. Given that she fled the scene after being caught, I'm willing to bet there's no such thing.

In short, I have every right to approach her.

After putting Jax to bed, I find Megan downstairs, reclined in the two-seater sofa with the

The Guest Bedroom

remote control on her lap. She's lazily hitting the buttons, flicking through the channels as images come and go so fast that the sound doesn't even kick in until she settles on an old episode of *Baywatch*. Not that she's watching – she focuses hard on gnawing her fingernails until she notices me, then stares over her knuckles as if I don't deserve to be there.

'What?' she asks.

'I saw you upstairs.'

'When?'

'Just now.'

'Impossible. I haven't moved.'

Sucking in a deep breath, I let it go in a sigh and move closer. It's important that I stand over her, hopefully intimidating her or at least letting her feel smaller than she seems to think she is. But even then, it doesn't seem to bother her in the slightest.

In fact, she doesn't move an inch.

'You *were* upstairs,' I say, trying not to let my voice break through nervousness. 'And don't try to deny it, because I saw you with my own two eyes.'

'Okay, fine.' Megan rolls her eyes. 'I was upstairs. So what?'

'I'd appreciate it if you kept to downstairs.'

'Why?'

'Because I said so, that's why.'

'Jesus, that's such a mum thing to say.'

'Yes, well, I'm a mum. It means I had to grow up.'

Megan snickers and continues biting her nails, then pretends to be even remotely interested in *Baywatch*. I absolutely despise this attitude of hers and, although I'm petrified that she'll let my secret get out if I push her too far, it doesn't mean she can walk all over me. This is my home, after all, and she's nothing more than a guest.

An *unwanted* guest.

She's acting like a disrespectful child, so I treat her like one. Moving fast as lightning, I lash forward and snatch up the TV remote, then hit the power button. Megan shoots upright to complain, but I point a finger right at her and start my lecture before she can get a word out.

'Listen up and listen well. This is *my* house, which means you play by *my* rules. If I tell you to keep entirely to the downstairs, that's exactly what you're going to do. What's more, if I tell you to back away from my kid, you back away. If you try telling my husband lies about my sexuality, you'll

The Guest Bedroom

be out on the street before you can ask what happened. Are we clear?'

Megan stares, her jaw hanging open while she sizes me up. Then she releases an awkward laugh that lasts all of two seconds. It seems as though she thinks I'm joking – that I'll start laughing along with her and drop the façade. Don't get me wrong though, it's tempting. This whole telling-off is tough to keep up when you're as nervous as I am.

'You're serious,' she says, discarding the laugh.

'As a heart attack. My way or the highway.'

'That's not a very nice way to treat your friend.'

'Who says we're friends?'

Once more, a look of utter shock. What planet is she living on? Does she really think I like her after everything she's done? Even her past sins are unforgivable, but to come to my home and start causing trouble when I'm trying to live my life?

No, it's better to stay strong.

Megan scoffs like a moody teenager and climbs up off the sofa, kicking in the recliner with a smack. As she passes me – too close for comfort, one might add – she mumbles something under her breath that instantly makes me shake with a cocktail of anger and fear. Then, before I know it, she slams the guest bedroom door and rocks the whole house.

Jordan comes in from the kitchen, paperback clutched in one hand while he hangs from the door frame with a furrowed brow and a slight scowl.

'What the hell was that noise?' he asks.

'Megan,' is all I say.

'Why is she slamming doors?'

'Because she's a little brat.'

'Wow. Want me to talk to her?'

'Definitely not.'

I leave on that note, going upstairs to stay far away from Megan if she chooses to resurface. I'd really like to keep her far away from Jordan, but I can't be overprotective. It's not a jealousy thing – my husband has always been fiercely loyal to me – but the longer she's around him, the more chance there is of her blabbing my little secret. Especially after I just had a go at her and put her in a place. I know what comes next, as I know her all too well.

She'll start scrambling for control.

THE NEXT COUPLE of days are even worse.

First, on the same night I tried to put Megan in her place, I awoke with a start to a banging sound. My eyes are barely open, but they strain to look at

The Guest Bedroom

the baby monitor. Relieved to see no harm has come to him, I sit up and tap Jordan lightly.

'Hey, are you awake?'

'Hardly.'

'Did you hear the crash?'

'No.'

'Well, there was one.'

'Ugh. Want me to check it out?'

No, I really don't. Jordan loves his sleep too much, and it's probably just my mind playing tricks on me. Anyway, if he's up and searching the house then he'll struggle to get back to sleep, then I'll have an angry husband to live with until he's fully rested again, and that might take days. It's definitely better I check this one out myself.

Half-asleep, I search the place from top to bottom. Nobody is here. Even in the dark, however, I do manage to see a splinter in the door frame of the guest bedroom. I sigh and shake my head, finally realising that my sleep was disturbed all because of Megan throwing a tantrum. I try not to let it bother me, then head back to bed.

The very next morning is no better. Megan lounges around the house like a kid, leaving a mess behind her, scoffing every time she sees me, and generally being a nuisance. She won't do it around Jordan, of course – no, that's when her entire attitude changes just to make me look like the bad guy. It's not even something I can dispute, because I know what pushing her buttons will end up doing to my life.

It would be catastrophic.

Another night goes by, and Megan drops my favourite mug. She pretends it was an accident and goes crying to Jordan, but it doesn't get to me like she hoped it would. I know what all of this is, because I've seen it all before. It's nothing more than pushback after telling her she's not allowed upstairs. I just don't get it though. It felt like she was creeping around the house, and it made me uncomfortable. What was I supposed to do?

My own home has become a very awkward place to live. Every little strop she throws leaves me feeling more and more like she's up to something. Why is she even here? It should be more than obvious that she's not welcome. There was a reason I left her in the past and never called her. If I wanted to speak to her ever again, I easily could have... probably. Surely, that should have been taken as a pretty strong hint?

Regardless, Megan is up to something. I can

The Guest Bedroom

feel it in my bones, and I'm not going to let my guard down until I know what it is. Maybe if she asks nicely, it's something I can give her. As long as it's not friendship, forgiveness, or money.

Oh, or my husband.

Chapter 6
Jordan

There's been a very distinctive change in my wife since Megan came along.

It's not a good change either. Her general mood has hit the ground, making her an extremely stressful person to be around. I've tried to undo some of that by treating her to flowers and paying extra attention to her when she talks.

Even when she talks about Megan.

That's all I seem to hear about these days. Don't get me wrong, I understand why having her in the house might be a tense situation for her, but Becca always had the option of tossing Megan on to the street. I must admit, it does make me curious that she's so unhappy with her 'friend' being in this

The Guest Bedroom

house, and yet she hasn't done a single thing to get rid of her.

She must be hiding something.

I've been getting little hints of a darker history between the two of them anyway. Over coffee, Megan started hinting at a physical relationship they shared years ago. Let me just clarify that I'm no idiot – I saw the relief on my wife's face when 'the big secret' was something as petty as a short-term gay experience. There was something much bigger that, for some reason, they both decided to hide from me.

The question is, what?

As if that little incident wasn't enough, Megan's started slamming doors. Becca has been getting more and more worked up by it, and I don't blame her. Jax is a very light sleeper – even a violent sneeze will wake him up screaming – and the crash of a door echoing through the house isn't going to help matters. Becca is already sleep-deprived as it is, so no wonder she's at her wits' end. It does spring a question back to the forefront of my mind though.

Why not just get rid of her?

It only strengthens my theory that something is

going on between them. You'd think, being a policeman, that I'd be inclined to get to the bottom of this mystery. But that's just the way I am – their business is their business, and I don't want any more drama.

Not after the time I've had in this town.

Collingwood is a small, neighbourly sort of place. As with most towns, we get the occasional ruffian stirring up trouble. In our case, the troublemaker was the boss's son, which only made things harder. While all of that chaos was causing political trouble, I made a firm decision to wipe my hands of all things dramatic, saving my energy for simply doing my job and being the best dad I can be. It's a juggling act, but we get through.

Still, I am curious...

It's not nice to snoop, so I'll let Becca keep her secrets. All I ask is that it's not something that will affect our marriage or the safety of our family. Not that I imagine it will do either of those – Becca is a good woman, and she would never bring trouble to our doorstep.

At least, I don't think so.

I'M TRYING NOT to stress out about all of this.

The Guest Bedroom

When I arrive home from work, the tension is so thick you can hack at it with a chainsaw and still not make a scratch. Megan is listening to music in the guest bedroom, her face buried in a laptop as she (hopefully) searches for a local job. She looks up and smiles at me, then waves with wiggling fingers. I smile and move on to find Becca in the kitchen with Jax.

This right here? It's the best part of my day.

I try to let go of work stresses when I'm at home. Becca often asks me to vent and blow off some steam, but today she looks too fed up and ready to go on holiday. Maybe I'll treat her to one when Megan is out of the picture. Though to be honest, the thought of her leaving does make my stomach sink, even if only a little.

When bedtime comes, Jax goes out like a light and Becca retires early. I join her, trying to enjoy my book while recent events course around my brain like cars on a racetrack. It's only been a couple of days, and it already feels like my wife is becoming a stranger. It keeps me up at night, long past when she falls asleep, and I'm determined not to waste time lying here when I could be enjoying a bit of quiet TV in the living room.

It's a good thing I have tomorrow off.

Downstairs, I stay as quiet as possible, making a cup of camomile tea and finding something that's exactly the right mix between an interesting show and something I don't need on at a high volume to enjoy. I settle for an old episode of *Top Gear*, but then barely get through a whole minute before someone coughs at my side.

I startle a little, craning my neck to see Megan leaning against the door frame. Her arms are crossed over a long, white nightie that I can see through. Did she put that on especially for me, I wonder a little too hopefully?

'Sorry, did I wake you?' I ask.

'Sort of, but it's okay. What are you watching?'

'Nothing special.' I flick off the TV and scoot over so she can sit beside me. She doesn't move, which confuses me a little. Whether or not I choose to act on them, she's giving me some weirdly mixed signals. It's a shame – I don't like to be played with.

'Are you coming in?' I ask.

'Me? No. Just checking to see what the noise was.'

'Well, sorry to disturb you.'

'Doesn't bother me. Hey, can I talk to you about something?'

The Guest Bedroom

'Sure.'

'I'm a little worried about Becca.'

'What do you mean?'

Megan shakes her head then lowers it, her luscious black hair falling down like curtains. When she looks up, she's biting her lip seductively, like a completely different person from who she was just a few short seconds ago.

'I mean, she seems a little stressed.'

'She's a stay-at-home mum,' I remind her.

'Okay, so she seems *really* stressed. How does she get time to please you?'

Something stirs in me – something I choose to ignore because it's the only safe way forward. I shift uncomfortably on the sofa, then rest my chin on my knuckles, hiding my interested expression behind my hand.

'You mean...?'

'Sexually, Jordan.'

'I don't know how that's any of your business.'

'Hmm.'

Megan smirks, then turns, her bare legs moving slowly, weightlessly, as she glides through the door without so much as a goodnight. Although she does say one thing before closing the door – something that does a thousand different things to me.

'I'm just putting it out there,' she says. 'You're overdue an upgrade.'

Chapter 7
Becca

First thing in the morning, I'm up and about to prepare things for Jax. We're going out today, heading to a huge outdoor park called Play Days, where they also serve hot food and coffee to keep the parents' energy up. We love it there, and so does our son.

Jordan had trouble getting up when I left him an hour ago, but he's soon on his feet and trying to help out. Last night was a late one, he tells me, explaining that he just couldn't settle so spent most of the night in the living room. This happens occasionally, and it makes me feel sorry for him, but this time I'm just glad Megan didn't exploit my weakness.

Let's just say she has a history of stealing men.

I'm only packing a large, family lunchbox when she comes sniffing around in the kitchen. With no interest in food at this time of the morning, she simply potters around in that nightie and lingers like a bad fart. I feel watched with every move I make, which encourages me to look her dead in the eye and question it.

'Do you need something?' I ask.

As usual, Megan is all thin-lipped smiles. 'No, thank you.'

'Then go find something to do. We're sort of busy.'

'Busy doing what?'

'Getting ready to go out. Not that it's any of your concern.'

Megan's eyes widen with shock and humour, but the smile doesn't alter. With that, she pushes herself away from the kitchen counter and wanders into the living room. Uncomfortable heat spikes my back at this – Jordan is in there with Jax, and I don't like leaving them alone together. Every second they're in the same room, my dark, dangerous secret could come out.

I quickly stash the last of the snacks into the lunchbox and stuff it in a bag. It takes a couple of minutes to finish getting things together, but we're

The Guest Bedroom

just about ready to go. I head into the living room, the big bag hanging off my shoulder, then stop short when I see Megan.

'What's wrong?' she asks.

We both know what's wrong – she's dressed in those same black jeans and the tight top, and now she's shrugging on her jacket like she's intending to come with us. I look to Jordan as he appears in the doorway, Jax babbling in his arms. It takes all of two seconds for him to pick up on the awkwardness in the room.

'Oh, Megan wants to come with us,' he says. 'Hope you don't mind.'

Megan gives an evil sneer then heads outside to wait by the car. My heart is pounding, my mood plummeting into sheer misery. This feels like a violation, and she knows it – it's probably the only reason she wanted to join us in the first place.

'I'm not comfortable with this,' I tell Jordan.

'With what?' he asks. 'Going out?'

'No, with *her* coming.'

'Why not?'

'It's *our* thing.'

'Oh, come on. It's just one time.'

'It's not, though, is it?' I sigh and go to the window in the hall, looking out at the driveway.

Megan is out there leaning against the car with one hand on it, eagerly awaiting our departure. 'She came along for coffee and cake, she joins us at every meal, and now we can't even have a day off together as a family.'

Jordan doesn't say anything. He rarely does when I'm upset, as he knows it's difficult to turn my mood around. Thankfully, he at least comes to my side, puts a hand on my shoulder, and whispers in my ear that he's sorry. I appreciate him doing that, and I'm not taking it personally, but it doesn't change how I feel about the situation.

Violated.

Play Days is set on the edge of Collingwood, a huge and inclusive park for children of all ages. There are giant wooden structures with climbing pegs and rope swings and enormous slides. As you go further back, you start to uncover the smaller zones with what can only be described as plastic igloos. These igloos have windows like a Wendy house, and they're surrounded by smaller slides with swings and a roundabout. It's not the quietest area – especially today, when the sun is shining – but Jax is going to love it.

The Guest Bedroom

Megan has rushed off ahead of us, walking like Miss Prim and Proper, her head tilted up to look at the surrounding woodland. The trees here are massive and resplendent with luscious green. There's a soft breeze to rustle the leaves, but it's not cold. It's actually the perfect day.

At least it would have been.

'How are you feeling now?' Jordan asks quietly, Jax writhing in his arms.

'It doesn't matter. There's not much we can do about it now.'

'Once again, I'm sorry. She just seemed... I don't know. Lonely.'

That doesn't surprise me in the slightest. Megan was always an in-your-face kind of person, which made it hard for her to find friends. When she struggled like that, she only tried harder and, in turn, became even more in-your-face. It was a downward spiral created by her desperation, and that spiral only led to sympathy.

No wonder she always got her own way.

When we finally arrive at the park, Megan is already ordering a round of coffees and some hot doughnuts. I find it suspicious that she would put her hand in her own pocket for us, especially when she's unemployed. It's not like I'll turn down a generous offer like that – seeing as she has already paid for it – but it still makes me feel like she's up to something.

'Can I ask you guys something?' she says when we settle down on the picnic bench.

I look to Jordan, who's already seeking approval from me. All I can do is nod.

'Well,' Megan goes on. 'I feel really bad for interrupting your family day, so I was wondering if you wouldn't mind me playing with Jax. That way you two can enjoy a nice hour or two together, maybe have a wander if you like, and I can keep the little one entertained.'

Jordan opens his mouth to speak, but I cut him off out of fear alone.

'That's not a great idea,' I tell the pair of them. 'We barely know you.'

'Come on,' Megan moans. 'We grew up together.'

'And I haven't seen you in years.'

'But I'm still the same person.'

That's what scares me. Most people discover themselves, improve themselves, and change. Only the narcissists stay the same person for years, and they're the most dangerous people on the planet. This narcissist in particular.

The Guest Bedroom

'Maybe... we should talk about it?' Jordan asks.

'I'll leave you two alone.'

Megan disappears, heading towards the play equipment as if to identify what she's about to use. Meanwhile, Jax sees all the fun things to do and continues to wriggle. Jordan struggles to keep hold of him, so I take over and realise he's just as chaotic with me.

'It could be worth it,' Jordan says. 'We rarely get time to talk any more.'

'I'm not about to trust her with our child.'

'Why not? What exactly do you have against her?'

'It's a long story.' I sigh and glance at Megan, who sees us and waves. It makes my skin crawl. 'At the end of the day though, I wouldn't press you to leave our son with someone you're not comfortable around. Is it really that much to ask for you to play by the same rules?'

Jordan sighs this time, reaching out with a half-smirk to playfully grab Jax's cheek. He lets go when there's some pushback. 'Actually, I understand and agree. But it is very rare we get time to talk while Jax is getting more and more excitable. So can I make a suggestion?'

'Go ahead...' Yes, I'm sceptical.

'Why not let her play with him as long as they're in sight at all times?'

'That's not a good idea.'

'Why not? Megan's happy, Jax is happy, and we can enjoy a snack in peace.'

It sounds tempting, but nothing in this world can make me trust that woman.

'What's the worst that can happen?' Jordan says. 'She can't go off anywhere without passing us, we'll have eyes on her the whole time, and it's not like Jax will go doing backflips off the tallest structure he can find. I'm just saying, to keep the peace...'

Before I can even reach a decision on the matter, Megan returns to us and starts the baby talk with Jax. He lights up around her, which breaks my heart because I want everyone else to see her the same way I do – as nothing more than trouble.

But Jordan does have a point. It can't hurt to lighten the load, as long as we stick to the rules he just outlined. It's not like Megan is a responsible human being, but these little displays of trust could go a long way to making us get along well again. That, in turn, could lead to me feeling comfortable around her, and knowing she won't have something against me.

The Guest Bedroom

That's the only reason I let it happen.

I just hope not to regret it.

SURPRISINGLY, nothing at all goes wrong.

Megan is actually great with Jax, escorting him down the slide and acting all goofy while Jordan and I watch from not too far away. To be honest, it's getting easier to believe that she's not the monster she always used to be. If erasing those sins is even remotely possible.

But for now, things are okay. Jax is safe, we can see the two of them, and Jordan holds my hand for the first time in a while. When I look at him, he smiles softly as if to assure me that everything is okay. And what's more is I believe it.

For now.

The next couple of hours fly by. Jax falls asleep in Jordan's arms as we begin the short walk back to the car and try transferring him into his seat. There's very little fuss, although it's a close call when Jordan manoeuvres our son's arm, and Jax stirs with his pudgy little cheeks moving from one seat belt to the next. I breathe a sigh of relief when he goes straight back to sleep, the straps secure and the seat clicked into position.

Jordan smiles as he closes the door softly and walks around the car, but Megan stays at my side. It feels like she wants something, but that only makes me wary. As soon as Jordan disappears behind the steering wheel and closes his door, Megan touches my arm.

'Thanks for letting me play with Jax,' she says. 'I know that was hard for you.'

I smile a little and am surprised to notice it's real. Could it really be that the monster has a sweet side? Some actual, genuine appreciation for the discomfort I just put myself through? I soften a little, not quite letting my guard down but not being a bitch either.

'You're welcome. And thank you for being so good with him.'

'That's okay. You and Jordan needed the time then, hey?'

'It's not what you think.'

'Not an unstable marriage?'

I pause, watching the smile slowly creep back into her witchlike features. She's trying to insinuate that Jordan and I are having a rocky relationship. Have we done something to make it seem that way, or is it wishful thinking on her part?

The Guest Bedroom

'There's nothing wrong with our marriage,' I tell her firmly.

'Oh. Okay, I just thought... Never mind.'

'No, go on.'

Megan shifts uncomfortably but still smiles like an evil ghost. 'It's just that sometimes you look at people and get a sense of their relationship, you know? Like, as soon as I saw you together, I knew there was a terrible secret between the two of you.'

'You know there is.'

'Oh, yes, and he can find out at any minute.'

A headache forms, burning my skull. Stress is the bullet, and Megan is the gun. If there was ever any doubt that she's here to cause trouble, that's gone the second she mentions my secret. I'm trying to put words together, stuck somewhere between wanting to beg her to stop and biting her head off. But before I can do either, she finishes me off.

'See, the only reason I took Jax off your hands is because it's better than the alternative.' She leans in then, sugary-sweet perfume assaulting my senses. Then comes the real hit – the part that makes me want to slap her. 'I could have just taken your husband instead.'

Chapter 8
Becca

Megan fully moves herself in over the next couple of days. I know she was already in our house, but now she's making herself at home. Think intrusively, or even invasively; there are black wisps in my hairbrushes, my toothbrush goes missing here or there then magically reappears, and my secret stash of chocolate bars seems to be shrinking by the day. I know it's her who's taking it – Jordan hates chocolate, and Megan is a plague upon our house.

Although all of that is infuriating, none of it is as bad as the fact she keeps making hints at unveiling my secret. Nor have I got over what she said about taking my husband away. I trust Jordan completely and am almost certain he would never

The Guest Bedroom

betray me, but that doesn't make it okay for her to try. Worst of all, it's not even like I can stop her or kick her out.

It's the secret she has over me.

The thing is, she has an equally bad secret. Actually, it's significantly worse. The thing I did is barely a blemish compared to the full-blown evil she committed herself. But that doesn't mean I can blurt it out. If I did, she would quickly reveal the truth about me and end my life as I know it. Basically, although I have a weapon, her weapon is bigger.

In spite of all this, I'm past the point of just letting her walk all over me. If she's going to stay in my home then the least she can do is stop with the threats. I plan to catch her alone at some point, but even that window is ever closing – Jordan is off for the weekend, and she clings to him like a needy puppy.

I do finally get the opportunity on Sunday morning, when Jordan is in the shower and Jax is taking his midday nap. Approaching Megan out of the blue is far from the safest option, but I'm done sitting by and taking it. It's my house, after all, which ultimately means my rules.

Joining her in the living room, where the

laptop wobbles on her thighs as she types away, I sit beside her on my own leg, facing her. It looks like she's in the zone, barely noticing me as she hammers away at the keys. Upstairs, the shower turns off and the house goes silent, the last of the water trickling through the pipes. The bathroom door opens, and Megan finally sees me.

My time is very limited.

'We need to talk,' I say to her calmly.

'What about?'

'All of these things you've been doing.'

'Like what?'

A brief sigh escapes me. It's clear how this is going to be, and I don't like it one little bit. My eyes dart to the clock, noting the time just to see how very little of it there is before Jordan comes down to interrupt us. In fact, I can hear his footsteps now, slowly creaking their way down the stairs as I rush to get the last of my words out.

'These threats, they need to stop.'

'What threats?'

'Don't be ridiculous. You know exactly what I'm talking about.'

Megan's smile deepens as Jordan appears in the doorway, his plain, comfortable clothing sticking to his still-damp body. Slick-black hair

The Guest Bedroom

clings to his forehead as he smiles in our direction, then takes a seat in the armchair and starts playing with his phone.

My chance is gone. Megan smirks at me, knowing she's just got away with my mellow approach. I'll have to find another opportunity if and when it comes along, but it can't be the same calm, civilised way I just did it. Jordan needs to be out of the house, and I'll have to assert myself just like my mother always insisted. As nervous as it makes me, I have to try.

Because the alternative terrifies me.

JAX IS ASLEEP EARLY TONIGHT, after having a super active day at the play gym. It leaves the three of us to talk a little over dinner, which Megan weirdly helped to prepare. She didn't talk to me the whole time, save for asking me how many vegetables to slice or how long to leave the oven on for. I found it truly bizarre that she wanted to help, but even more so that she did so without engaging in conversation with me. I wanted to reopen yesterday's little chat, of course, but it was difficult with Jordan coming in and out.

Now that we're seated around the table, all

tucking in to a chicken dinner that smells like hot potatoes and melted butter, I feel slightly more at ease. Megan can give me as many dirty looks as she likes, but I'm on to her.

Remember, I know about her, too.

Halfway through the meal, Jordan gets up to fetch a bottle of red wine we got from some subscription service. He pours three big glasses and sits back down, smiling at the pair of us as if everything is okay. But Jordan is smarter than he lets on. He knows better.

'I was thinking,' he says, collecting his cutlery again. 'Perhaps I should take Jax out for the day and give you two a chance to catch up. We did kind of thrust ourselves into this situation, and you haven't even been able to relax for even a minute. Not with Megan's job search and Becca's day-to-day care.'

Megan glares at me across the table. 'That's a great idea. Don't you think?'

Naturally, I shrug. 'Life is kind of busy. Chores need doing.'

'I'll handle those, too,' Jordan tells me.

'Yeah, but—'

'Come on.' Megan bites her lip, enjoying every second of this. 'We can have a girls' day, hang out

The Guest Bedroom

all day long and talk about all that's happened these past few years. I mean, if you prefer, we could just catch up right now, right in front of Jordan.'

I shake my head and put a slice of chicken in my mouth, tasting nothing but bitter anger. Whatever the hell Megan is up to, it's clear she's not trying to reform like she says she is. Every word she chooses is a deliberate move to upset me. But why? It's like she wants me to slip up, or maybe she just enjoys torturing me with her knowledge. Once again, I remind myself that I'm not the only one with a secret. If hers gets out...

'Becca?' Jordan says. 'You've gone quiet.'

'She's just thinking it through,' Megan says. 'That's smart.'

'What is there to think about?'

I look up from my plate, forcing the chicken down my throat. It's like swallowing a rock. 'What would we even do? It's not like there's anything to do in Collingwood other than take Jax somewhere. We'd have to leave town to find something.'

'Sounds good to me,' Megan says, reaching for her wine. 'Road trip?'

'*Road trip?*' I can barely believe my ears. 'Where? Why? How long for?'

'I think she just means for the day,' Jordan explains. 'Right?'

Megan takes a sip of her wine, then studies it approvingly. 'Well, I don't know about you, but I don't see any reason why we shouldn't do this. It will be just like the old days; a solid, uninterrupted conversation, a few giggles, maybe get our nails done. Sound good?'

'I really don't think—'

'Please, Becca. I'll even pay for everything.'

The way they're both looking at me feels like an attack. I can think of nothing worse than spending a whole day with Megan goddamn List, and the pair of them are doing a great job at pressuring me into it. How long can I resist before she starts making more threats?

I barely ask myself that before she answers it in her own special way.

'It will have to stay between us though, won't it?' Megan smirks like a proud little brat again. 'I mean, we'll have a chance to talk about all of our private things, including the past and what we're going to do about it. Otherwise, Jordan will be privy to our secrets, and we wouldn't want that to happen, would we?'

The mere mention of our secrets makes my

blood run cold. That devilish grin has me pinned. My husband is only a few feet away, hearing every word but not really knowing the true meaning behind them. It won't take much for Megan to wreck everything, and that's why – sadly – there's nothing I can do to fight this.

'Fine,' I say. 'But only for the day.'

Somewhere within the next twenty-four hours, Megan manages to convince Jordan to let her drive. On the condition I don't appeal, of course, which I'm not likely to do with everything at stake. Megan knows this, too, and uses it to her advantage with mocking puppy-dog eyes.

The sun is shining again today, but this time there's a bitter wind that whips against the windscreen. The road is long, straight, and smooth, with nothing but a torturous day ahead of us. Apparently, we're going to get our nails done, visit the cinema, then grab lunch just like best friends often do. Obviously, we're not best friends.

Anything but.

'I'm so glad we could find a way to make this happen,' Megan says, taking her eyes off the road for far too long so she can watch me while she talks. 'It was starting to feel a little stressful at home, wasn't it? What with all the confusion.'

'Confusion?' I'm gripping the armrest. 'What confusion?'

'You seem to think I'm threatening you. Victim complex, much?'

I roll my eyes, then point at the road to tell her to concentrate. Thankfully, she starts paying attention to what's ahead of us, which enables me to relax at least a little bit. There is an awkwardness in the car, however. One I'm unable to get over.

Even with that in mind, I promised myself I wouldn't let her walk all over me. So I turn my head and stare back, letting her feel my stare. Knowing the power she has over me, I'm worried about my throat locking up as I talk. I have to be brave about this.

'Let's not play head games then,' I say. 'We both know what's happening here, and it's giving me a headache. Why don't you just tell me what you want and then get on your way? Nobody needs to pretend you *want* to be here, and I don't have to pretend I'm okay with it.'

'Wow. I'm offended,' she mocks.

'You should be. There's a reason I don't like you.'

The Guest Bedroom

'So what? Nobody asked you to like me.'

'Cut the crap, will you? Why are you here?'

'That's my own business. Why are you being so rude?'

'Because I'm getting tired of you threatening me!'

Out of nowhere, Megan slams on the brakes. My body swings forward, but my head snaps back as the seat belt catches me. The car swerves, then comes to an abrupt halt on the side of the road. I catch my breath, or try to, but Megan turns in her seat with the Devil in her eyes and the shadow of sheer mania in her angry mouth.

'You want to cut the crap?' she barks. 'Fine, let's do that. First of all, you know damn well that all it will take to spill the beans on your best-kept secret is for me to say what happened and point at the evidence. I don't care if that brings me down with you, because I'll only blab if you don't give me what I want, and if I don't have that then who cares what happens to me?'

Terror grips me, but I try to put on a brave face. *Try*.

'What is it you want?' I ask weakly.

'Do you really have to ask? Think about it – what is the worst thing I could ever take away from you? What's the one thing that you'd struggle to let go of, even if it means going to prison for a long, long time?'

'You can't mean...'

'Yes, I do.' Megan touches her stomach. 'I can't have kids of my own, and I always wanted to be a mother. The agencies won't let me adopt – something to do with my mental health diagnoses, which is a load of crap – and my body doesn't work like it should. If I want a child, I'm going to have to get one using my own methods.'

I feel sick. The world won't stop spinning. Bile rises in my throat as I fight the urge to lash out and hit her. How dare she make demands like this. *How bloody dare she!*

'Now, just in case we're unclear,' she says. 'You're going to give me your son. Jax will become my own child, and the first thing I'll do with him is change that ridiculous name. Meanwhile, you're going to report him missing and claim to have no idea what happened to him. Maybe I'll see you on the news, crying for the cameras and begging 'whoever took him' to return him safely. And if you don't agree to all of this?'

I know what happens if I don't agree.

'On the other hand, I am generous. It's a big

decision to make, so I'm going to give you a whole week to make your decision. Until then, we're just going to have to play happy families. Do you understand what I'm saying to you, Becca?'

It pains me to no end, but I have to nod. As if my week wasn't going badly enough, now this psychopath is threatening to take my son away. The bare thought of living a life without Jax makes me sick to my stomach, and to know she could get away with it...

'See, I own you,' she says, turning back in her seat and bringing the engine back to life. 'Now, let's go and have a nice day, shall we? You know my terms and, if you care even a little bit about not getting locked up for the rest of your life, Jax will be mine within seven days.'

I can't speak. I can't think. Too many thoughts are racing through my mind. Even as the car moves on towards the neighbouring town, far away from where Jordan is taking care of our only child, I've never felt such fear for the safety of my family. It's like Megan said – she owns me, and she's given me a choice.

All I have is seven days.

Chapter 9
Becca

THAT DAY I spent with Megan was nothing short of torture.

She acted as if nothing had happened – as if she didn't just unveil her plans to steal my son, her knowledge of my big secret being her bargaining chip. I actually feel guilty for not laying into her, giving her an earful and telling her to get the hell away from my family. It was cowardice that kept me so quiet, I suppose. Plain, pathetic cowardice.

At least I didn't befriend her. Even with all her smiles and her offer to buy me lunch, I couldn't bring myself to give her anything more than a disgusted snarl. But Megan seemed to almost enjoy those pained expressions. It was like she knew the

The Guest Bedroom

pain she was causing and was actually *enjoying* it. That's the Megan I know.

The monster.

Anyway, that was yesterday. Today I'm staying home and keeping Jax close to me at all times. Even during his midday nap, I stay in the chair at his side, gently rocking back and forth while nibbling away at my fingernails and admiring my precious boy. I try to think of a life without him, but I can't even imagine it, much less go through with it. His messy little clump of blond hair ruffles over his puppy-fat face, an adorable frown resting on his forehead.

My little man, I think as my chest grows tight. *Nobody can take you away from me.*

I'm wrong, of course. Megan has every ounce of power over me. Whatever I choose to do, Jax will be out of my life for good. Believe me, I'm trying to think of a third option, but nothing is coming. Megan knows this, too, and that's probably why she feels so confident.

When Jax wakes up, I change his dirty nappy and make my way downstairs, where Megan is sprawled out on the sofa with one of my old magazines spread over her face. She looks up when I enter, smirks, then drops her head back down to the cushion. I don't want to be around her – that's the last thing I want – so I carry my son into the kitchen without a word.

'Not going to say hello?' Megan says snidely from the sofa.

I elect to ignore her, because she's only trying to wind me up. It's working, but I try to put it past me and focus on giving Jax a fruit bowl for a snack, dropping a few dry Cheerios in there as he seems to enjoy them so much. It feels safer out in the kitchen, so I might just stay here until Jordan gets home from work.

God, I wish I could tell him about our situation. Would he understand if I just revealed my past and begged his forgiveness? Or would the cop in him start asking questions, digging so deep that he would only regret it when he discovers who he married?

I'm deluding myself. Telling him isn't even an option. Telling *anyone* would be a grave mistake. This is something that must stay between Megan and me, even if it does bring my life to a crashing halt in just seven days.

Six days, I remind myself.

Six days and counting...

. . .

The Guest Bedroom

When my husband does eventually return from a long day at work, he kicks off his shoes and takes Jax right out of my hands. I watch them carefully, admiring the way they are with each other. It doesn't take much for Jordan to make him laugh hysterically, and it's the best sound in the world. For a moment, my worries melt away and that sound is all there is.

Until I see Megan snooping.

'How was work, babe?' she asks as if her own man just walked in the door.

'Fine, thanks.' Jordan looks over at me, discomfort causing lines on his face. 'Anything to report, Becca? Little Man eating okay, sleep okay, do lots of idle-widdle fart bubbles?'

As Jax starts laughing at Jordan's stubble grazing against his cheek, Megan stares at me like some kind of animal. I know what she's doing, and she *wants* me to know. This is yet more control she has over me, and she's enjoying every last second.

'Can I talk to you alone?' I ask.

'I don't mind overhearing,' Megan says.

'Unfortunately, it's none of your business.'

'Ooh, so cold.'

Jordan looks from one of us to the other, clearly picking up on there being some kind of problem.

He stops playing with our son and holds him close to his chest, then nods his head towards the stairs. 'Let's talk upstairs while I get ready for a shower.'

I follow him up, not looking at Megan as I pass but feeling her eyes all over me like a disease. I even get a waft of her cheap perfume, then make my way upstairs while trying not to gag. It's Megan all over – it seems sweet at first, but it'll mess with your senses.

Jordan is waiting for me in the bedroom, playfully dumping Jax on to the bed and briefly tickling his tummy. Jax squeals with delight, and I go to sit with him while Jordan moves around the room to prepare for his after-work shower. His back is to me the whole time.

'You wanted to talk?' he says.

'Not about anything in particular.'

'What's wrong?'

'It's just... Megan.'

'She's tripping over your toes?'

'You heard her down there. She was talking as if you're *her* husband.'

Jordan looks over his shoulder, deadpan. 'But I'm not.'

'You don't think I know that?' A sigh leaves my tight chest. 'Nothing has been the same since she

The Guest Bedroom

arrived, and it hasn't even been that long. It's starting to feel like it's her home and I'm the guest. It's not right, and I don't know what to do about—'

Jax leaps into my lap, playing with the buttons on my cardigan. I catch him, make sure he's safe, then avert my gaze to Jordan as he turns on the en-suite shower and returns to the bedroom, ripping off his shirt to reveal the abs that have slowly been turning to fat ever since our child was born. I think they call that a dad bod.

'You can always make her leave,' he says. 'I'll even do it for you.'

'That's not really a good idea.'

'Why's that?'

I utter an exasperated laugh. It's not something I can explain, not even to the man I married – the man I love with all my heart and vowed to share everything with. Everything except the sins of my past, that is. It makes me feel sick with myself.

'Becca...' Jordan comes in, drops his shirt, then looks me in the eye.

'Yes?'

'Are you hiding something?'

A dry lump forms in my throat. 'Why do you ask?'

'You've just been very different since Megan arrived.'

'Well, yeah, I'm uncomfortable.'

'It's more than that, isn't it?'

I don't say anything, mostly because I don't like lying to him. Thankfully, Jax starts giggling right on time. I look away from Jordan and, in time, he gives up to take his shower. Don't get me wrong, it's tempting to go in and blurt the truth – maybe he can help with the situation – but the risk is too great. My entire life could fall apart before my six days are up.

Scooping Jax into my arms, I carry him into his playroom.

It's the safest room in the house.

EARLY THAT SAME EVENING, things go from bad to worse.

I'm in the kitchen with Jax (a scene that's becoming far too familiar, but at least it's away from all the craziness). Megan is in the downstairs guest bedroom again, the door wide open as she obnoxiously blares distorted nineties tunes from her laptop speakers. The song selection isn't lost on me either – they're all from an era when the two of

The Guest Bedroom

us were best friends. Before the switch flipped inside of her, taking away the sane, rational woman I once adored.

Jordan is coming in and out of the house and leaving the front door wide open while he tinkers with the car. I'm not even sure what he's doing – the science of motor engineering goes way over my head – but he finds it therapeutic to constantly tweak it. I don't mind, as long as he doesn't make it blow up or something.

Honestly, I'm still just trying to process our last conversation. Jordan comes inside and wipes something off with a rag, smiling at me from the doorway that leads to the hall. I smile back, wondering how I can tell him the truth. It's the only secret I have from my husband, but even the thought of spilling the beans makes something inside me twist with anxiety.

As soon as he's out of sight, returning to the family car once more, Megan emerges from the bedroom. I should have noticed the music stopping, but I've been so wrapped up in entertaining my son as he munches on cut-up melon. Just watching him attack that task makes my heart swell with pride, but now there's a literal shadow looming over me.

'How's my little man this morning?' Megan asks.

That knot in my stomach tightens. 'I think you'll find he's *my* little man.'

'Yeah, we'll see.'

Jordan shuts the front door then. The temperature changes in the kitchen. It should be warmer, but Megan's presence leaves an icy chill in the air. A moment later, all four of us are in the kitchen, the silence growing more and more unsettling.

'Whoa,' Jordan says. 'Who died?'

'Nobody.' Megan lays a hand on my shoulder. 'I was just asking Becca if I can hold Jax for a little while, but she's being very untrusting. Some parents do tend to get a little overprotective, but I know what I'm doing.'

'You do?'

'I have nieces and nephews.'

That's a lie, but I don't call her on it. Instead, I just look up at Jordan and pray he can see the discomfort in my eyes. He does look, but it doesn't seem to register – he's too distracted by the motor grease on his hands, which he moves to wash in the sink. When he dries them with a dish towel and throws it into the washing machine, he inspects the

The Guest Bedroom

cleanliness and lifts Jax from his high chair with strong ease.

'What do you think?' he asks our son. 'Want Megan to hold you for a while?'

'No bloody way!' The words come out of my mouth before I've even thought them through. I shoot out of my chair and reach for Jax. Jordan steps back, taking him out of my grasp. Desperation urges me to get closer, trying again, but Jordan snaps at me.

'Will you stop? What's your problem?'

'I told you I'm not comfortable with it.'

'Why so protective?'

'Because he's our child, for crying out loud. It's my job.'

'Right? And what's Megan going to do, run away with him?'

Megan snickers behind me. If only Jordan knew how close to the truth he is. I shake my head, closing my eyes while tears sting them. Calmly, slowly, I reach out one more time and plead him to just let go. It's a weird feeling – he's studying me while I take hold of Jax, seeing this version of me for the first time. I don't hold it against him. It probably does look like I'm overreacting, but he has no idea of the monster living in our home.

Jax has no complaints about me taking him. I turn on the spot and feel anxious about walking past Megan. She's still standing there, grinning like an idiot and refusing to step aside to grant me an easy exit. Just as I head out the door, I catch Jordan apologising to her as if I'm the one in the wrong. As if *I'm* the psychopath.

'It's fine,' Megan says. 'She's having a hard time post-partum.'

Pure hatred rages in me all over again. I go upstairs to start Jax's bedtime routine a little early, mostly because I just want to stay the hell away from downstairs. As I run the bath and start getting out the rubber fish, I keep thinking about how fast the second day has flown by. After I've gone to sleep and woken up, it will be just five more days.

Then my life will be over.

Chapter 10
Jordan

As you can imagine, I found that very confusing.

Did I push the boundary with Becca by offering our son to Megan? Yeah, probably. We all make mistakes, and I'm not too proud to say that was one of mine. That said, was it really bad enough to warrant that reaction – snatching Jax and storming out?

It's extremely awkward after that. Megan's eyes meet mine just long enough to let me know she's upset about the outburst, then looks away. I feel guilty towards the both of them, having ignored my wife's wishes and then letting Megan see the explosion it caused.

This needs fixing.

I apologise briefly to Megan and then head upstairs. Becca is kneeling beside the bath, lukewarm water spilling into the tub while Jax smashes two rubber fish together on the carpet beside her. This is a stressful time for us – Jax hates water and lets everyone know about it with his deafening wails – so I roll up my sleeves, shut the door, and kneel beside Becca.

'Want to tell me what that was about?' I ask.

She doesn't look at me. She's busy swishing water around the bath to level the temperature, adding bubbles in a desperate attempt to make it more fun for Jax. I watch her chest heave up and down as she sighs. I've seen this look before. There's something she's not telling me, and I'm growing more curious as to what it is.

'I told you I wasn't comfortable with Megan holding him,' she says moodily.

'Yeah, but why not?'

'It doesn't matter why. I said not to, and you tried to force it anyway.'

'Is it really that big of a crime? You were happy with them playing in the park.'

'Well, that was before.'

'Before *what*?'

Becca shakes her head and huffs when stop-

The Guest Bedroom

ping the water. I pick up Jax, who's already unclothed and ready for his happy splash, then gently lower him into the tub. Becca's phone has some songs playing by animated fruit, which distracts him long enough to at least wash his back. That's as far as we get before he gets bored, starts screaming again, and the chaos unfolds.

We don't get another chance to talk about what happened downstairs, and the lack of closure doesn't sit well with me. Still, for as long as our son is watching, my displeasure isn't an emotion I wish to display. So I make use of our time as a family, putting bubbles on my face to try making him smile, the overpowering strawberry fragrance burning my nasal passages. Somehow, I get a giggle out of him that last two seconds.

That's better than nothing.

As soon as we're done, Becca and I work together just as we always have: in perfect, silent coordination to get the job done. We're a great couple, happy at even our worst moments, but that doesn't mean I'm not suspicious. I have every right to be, because the woman in front of me isn't the same one I married. No, this one is anxious, angry, and hiding something.

It's only a matter of time until I find out what.

. . .

Feeling a little run-down from my full-time job and the bizarre new stresses at home, I return downstairs and flick the kettle on, ready to make myself a coffee. I might even put a little something-something in it just to spice things up. It feels sorely needed.

Becca has retired to the bedroom for a while. She says it's to read her book, but she's a lazy reader just like I was not so long ago. If I know her (which I obviously do), she'll have the paperback resting on her lap while she scrolls through social media and just kills time. Not that I blame her – it must be tiring doing what she does all day. If anyone deserves a break, it's her.

The water bubbles, steam rising from the spout. The button clicks, and I rub my eyes before melting the instant coffee granules, avoiding milk altogether. The stronger the drink, the better. At least for right now.

'Making one for me, honey?'

The voice catches me off guard. The words don't match the person who said them. I spin around and find Megan standing just a few inches from me. I can smell her sugary-sweet perfume,

The Guest Bedroom

like summer threw up on a bowl of citrus fruits. It might entice a teenager, but all it does is help keep my more natural inclinations at bay. It's just as well – I'm not a cheater.

'Sorry, did you want a coffee?' I ask.

'Only if you're making it.'

'Who else would do it?'

Smiling, I turn back around and reach for a second mug, then quickly put together a drink for our guest. When I slide it on to the counter for her, she smiles thinly and takes a shrugging breath. Something is bothering her. I can see it.

'Can we talk about something?' she asks as if reading my mind.

'Again? What's on your mind?'

'It feels like Becca has been really moody with me since I arrived. There's a little bit of rough history between us – don't know if she told you – but I was hoping she'd overlook it just like I did. Has she said anything to you?'

I shrug uncomfortably. 'It's not really my business.'

'Fair enough, but she's your wife. I don't want to upset her. Or you, for that matter.'

'You're not upsetting me. But whatever this thing is between you, it needs resolving.'

'That might be awkward.' Megan wrings her fingers and averts her gaze. 'I tried talking to her about it, but she shut me down. It's like she has no interest in repairing our friendship. Honestly, if she's communicated that to you at all, could you please just tell me? At least then I could pack my bag and get out of everyone's hair.'

Sympathy makes my heart palpitate. 'You don't need to leave.'

'But it might be best. You saw how she reacted when I tried to hold Jax.'

'Maybe she's just going through some stuff.'

'Hmm. You're probably right.'

The kitchen becomes silent. I don't like the space between us. Not physically – there's only about ten inches, and even that suddenly vanishes when she rushes forward and throws her arms around me. Her perfume attacks my senses as she grips me so hard. It's like nobody has hugged her in years. If only for the sympathy, I hold her for a few seconds and let her know the world isn't out to get her. I'm here for her, to an extent.

Until she presses herself firmly against me.

Too close, I think, but I don't move.

Way too close.

Chapter 11
Becca

THIS KIND of tension is new to me.

I've lost my appetite, sleep is even harder to come by than before, and I don't even feel comfortable walking around my own home. Since Jordan has to leave for work again, it means I'm stuck at home with the psychopath who wants to take my child away.

It goes without saying that I'll be keeping my distance from her as long as possible but, weirdly enough, Megan doesn't seem interested in hanging out with me – she spends the whole morning in her room, the door wide open without her so much as blinking when I go past. Her head is buried in a book as she lies on the bed, the pages akimbo as she takes it all in. It's like she doesn't have a care in the world, and that only amplifies my cold fear.

It means she knows she'll get what she wants.

Around lunchtime, I try putting Jax down for his nap. It takes ages to get him settled, using his brain toys and a handful of his favourite books to make him sleepy. My own eyes are watering with painful fatigue as I tell him the story about a lion who's scared of a mouse, putting all my effort into performing it like a Broadway show. Eventually, he starts to yawn (just like I do), and then I transfer him to the cot and sneak out of the room.

As soon as the door is closed, I breathe a sigh of relief. That's the hard part done. Now, I just have to figure out whether to sneak in a nap of my own or get some chores ticked off my list. I opt for the latter, based solely on the fact that sleeping is tough right now. Although at least Megan has stopped slamming doors just to wind me up.

No, today she has a new tactic.

It starts in the living room, where I thought it might be safe to tidy for a few minutes before it all starts up again. I'm vaguely aware of the proximity to the guest bedroom, but there's no hide nor hair of Megan until she suddenly appears in the doorway. While the TV mumbles in the background, I watch her walking slowly around the room, examining the mantelpiece, then the framed pictures on the shelves, then finally ending up on the window seat. She sits there in her tattered old tracksuit, staring out down our long driveway.

'Do you have to watch my every move?' she asks.

'Of course,' I snap. 'It's not like you can be trusted.'

'Get over yourself. It's not like I'm going to steal anything. I just want my son.'

My stomach churns at the sound of those words. *'My son.'* All I can think in this twister of mortified thoughts is: *'No, you bitch, Jax is* my *son.'* Somehow, I manage to keep quiet after that, and I can tell it bugs Megan because she keeps huffing and stirring to get my attention. I know what she's doing – she's applying pressure to force me into a decision.

It's not going to happen.

She seems to have forgotten that I've seen all of this before. I used to go over to her house for dinner when we were kids. Megan would beg for dessert, and she wouldn't always get it. That's when the tantrums would start, and she would threaten to start destroying things. It's not like her mother could stop her – all she could do was send her to her bedroom, where she would destroy even more things. No wonder that poor lady turned to alcoholism and – word on the street is – eventually killed herself.

Megan gives up and storms into the kitchen with one last huff. Perhaps she expected me to follow her, because a few minutes later she comes back out and breezes right past me, then heads into the guest bedroom and slams the door. All this is after she makes one last comment – one more insane babble of words just to get a rise out of me.

'Can't wait to see my son again.'

Anger boils my blood. I suddenly realise I'm grinding my teeth, but the door is shut before the words really register. My eyes drop down to the baby monitor, where Jax stirs before drifting back off to sleep. *My little angel,* I think with a worried sigh.

That's the key phrase in all of this.

My little angel.

As soon as Jax wakes up and I get him fed, we sit around in his room while he ambles around and plays with one toy after the other. I'm so proud of

The Guest Bedroom

him for crawling, even if it is a lazy, almost limp manoeuvre from his belly. Other mothers tell me how fast this stuff goes, and that only makes me more scared about what could happen in the coming days.

Soon, he may not even be mine.

Once more, I punish myself with thoughts of Megan taking my child away. It infests my brain like a parasite, feeding off my thoughts until I start to go crazy. There's no way I can relax in this house. Not when I know she's just downstairs. That's when I decide to go and get some air, just for the intention of processing my emotions.

It only takes five minutes to get Jax in the buggy and ready to go. I wear the backpack that's just used for nappy changes and, although we won't be stopping anywhere long enough to need it, it's better to be safe than sorry. I also cram a couple of his favourite soft biscuits in there, along with a banana and a pineapple stick. The latter is for emergencies only – he loves sucking on a juicy pineapple, but the excited shrieking usually starts soon after. It's a trade-off I at least want the option of using if things get desperate.

At least Collingwood is a nice, quiet town. I'm able to think clearly out here, walking in the sun where a light breeze keeps me cool. It's that awkward time of year where spring is trying to turn into summer but not quite managing to. Some people get annoyed by the constant ups and downs in temperature, but I don't mind.

Besides, I have other things going on.

Jax enjoys his snacks while his curious head turns to the birds flying overhead and the occasional passing car. There's a long country road that leads up to the town proper, with huge fields on either side. Cows and sheep graze these fields, which also keep Jax's attention away from the soft biscuit he's insistent on sucking to death. A small tear emerges in the corner of my eye as I glance down at him, praying I don't lose him.

I just don't know what to do about Megan. She has my secret, and that's awful, but could anything really be as bad as taking my son? There's not even any evidence to suggest that she won't get what she wants and then reveal the truth anyway. God knows she's the type of person to do just that, which makes me think of just calling her bluff and letting her at it.

As if that could end well.

There's something else that keeps bugging me. I'm a mother, and I like to think I'm a good one, so

The Guest Bedroom

it does occur to me that this isn't about me at all. If you really think about it, the options aren't just about whether or not I end up in prison, but what will happen to him. If I let Megan have her way, Jax will lead a highly unsafe life under the care of a woman who can't even take care of her own basic needs. This makes it pretty clear to me that there really is only one thing to do, and that is to simply tell her no.

What will happen to Jax then?

There has to be another option. I wrack my brain while we take a tour of Collingwood in the half-summery sun. People pass and I offer thin smiles. The town is nice and quiet today, allowing me to consider something that just popped into my head. Something dangerous.

Because maybe I don't just have two choices after all. What if Megan is simply exploiting my kind nature and relying on me doing what she wants? What if I challenge her and let her know she'll be getting nothing from me? *Nothing.* On top of that, I'll be bringing her down with me. Surely, she can't be okay with that happening? Surely, she's as scared as me?

That's it. My mind is made up. It's not going to be easy, but Megan is about to be told that she'll *not* be getting what she wants. Not this time. What's more, she can pack her bags and leave today, as long as I'm aware of the potential outcome – that she can scream my secret from the rooftops and then leave town and never be seen again.

That's just a risk I'll have to take.

THE FAKE CONFIDENCE I'm giving off is ridiculous. My head is held high as I come in the door, parking the buggy in the hallway while Jax dozes once again. On any normal day I would prevent him from sleeping again because this will certainly mess with his night-time routine, but the additional few minutes this gives me will help an awful lot.

It's time to confront Megan.

My nerves are frayed as I search through the house. I'm starting to think she's stolen some things and run away – a loss that would honestly help me more than it would hurt me – but then I'm unlucky enough to find her roaming the upstairs hallway.

'What are you doing up here?' I ask.

Megan sneers at me. 'Whatever I want.'

'No, I told you to stay downstairs.'

The Guest Bedroom

'And *I* told *you* I'll do whatever I want. Are you going to stop me?'

There's a challenge in her eyes. She *wants* me to try stopping her, and she knows damn well it's not on the cards. I never was much of a fighter, and incidents from my younger years have only encouraged my pacifism, so I'm not likely to lunge out at anyone. Much less Megan, who has a... well, let's say a history of violence.

'That's what I thought.' Megan slides her hands into her jeans pockets and strolls right past me. It looks like she's going for the stairs, returning to her designated area after getting caught, but then she breezes past and starts looking at the pictures on the wall that leads only to our marital bedroom. She points at a photo. 'Who's this old bag?'

'That's my mother.'

'I remember her looking younger than that.'

'Time does that to a person.' My anxiety is sky-high. I try not to make my short, panicked breathing audible – Megan doesn't deserve the satisfaction. Anyway, it's time I put on a display of faux confidence and put her straight. 'You're going to have to leave.'

Still smiling, Megan rotates her head, then

looks me up and down. She opens her mouth as if to speak, then deliberates on it. A few long, uncomfortable seconds later, she walks slowly and casually towards me, not stopping until we're nose to nose, her foul breath invading my space while she stares daggers at me. Her smile fades.

'I'm not going anywhere,' she says firmly.

I lick my lips despite trying not to. My legs are shaking, my mouth bone dry. I'm scared to speak in case my voice breaks, but now she's put me on the spot. It's time to be brave. Assertive. Like my mother always told me to be.

'No,' I begin. 'This is my home, and you've taken advantage of—'

In the blink of an eye, Megan's hand lashes out like a whip. It strikes my chest, shoving me back. I lose my balance and fall against the wall. Photos fall to the floor, the glass frames shattering. She's on me then, like a tiger pouncing on its prey. Her hand snaps out again, this time clamping around my throat. I make a weird gargling sound as time seems to slow down and, somehow, speed up at the same time.

'Let me make one thing clear,' she hisses through her teeth. 'When I said I'm going to take my baby from you, I meant every word. When I

The Guest Bedroom

gave you a week to decide, I was being generous. Right now, when I tell you to *never* speak to me like that again, it's because I have some anger management issues and there's no telling what I'll do next. Got it?'

I try to nod, but her grip is so tight. Breathing becomes this impossible thing, so I reach up and try to prise her hand off my throat. It doesn't work. Megan sees I can't answer her, then lets go as I gasp for breath, doubling over like I'm about to faint.

'Don't make me do that again,' she says. 'Next time, it might get even worse.'

I'm left there in the hallway like a fool. Jax starts to make noises downstairs, probably woken by the commotion. I hate that it takes me a minute before I can get to him. It makes me feel like a failure as a mother, but nothing – *nothing* – can be worse than what will happen in five days, when Megan gets her own way.

And I'm too damn scared to do anything about it.

Chapter 12
Becca

Another day has dawned, which leaves only four.

My head is throbbing at the thought of it, although I did manage to get a few hours of semi-decent sleep. That's the exhaustion catching up to me, I think. It's just as well – even though Jordan is off work today, there are so many bits he has to do around the house that Jax is still going to need me at his every beck and call.

Bright and early, Jordan is out in the back garden drilling into something. Don't ask me what he does – I just make sure I thank him for keeping the house looking good while I take care of our son. It's easy to take people like him for granted, so I always make the effort to let him know he's appreciated by cooking for him. Although today will be a little different.

Today I'm busy looking for a way out.

Jax comes into my bedroom with me, where I set him down with one of his favourite toys – a fluffy, white bear which I'm only now realising must have been a festive thing. The scarf is a dead giveaway. Jax sits and cuddles it, examining the bear's little black nose while I pull out the drawer from under my bed and produce a faded yellow folder that's so light it's like there's nothing in it. That's by design – there *is* something inside, but I didn't want Jordan to feel a heft and then let curiosity get the better of him.

I take a deep breath to prepare myself, shoot one last glance at the door to ensure it's shut properly, then pull out the small collection of newspaper clippings. They fall into my hand, air-light and faded over time. The black ink feels weird and soft as it smudges my palm, but I'm more concerned about my hands shaking. Maybe I wasn't ready for this after all.

But I'm here now, and it's worth looking.

The article in the clipping speaks of a young woman who went missing in Bristol. My eyes skim over it, reading but not quite taking in the words because the last thing I want to do is relive that nightmarish day. Megan was there, too – she was always present when danger was – but it honestly seems like she has no regrets about what happened that day.

As I read on, the journalist talks about the police investigation, the enquiries made to those who were thought to be involved in the unfortunate event, and I read my maiden name as if it belonged to a different woman. Technically, it did – a fun-loving, carefree young lady died that day. Years later, desperate not to become this empty husk, she's sitting here reading about her past and hoping against hope that an idea springs to mind.

Thankfully, it does.

I start to wonder if I might get away with this legally. The obvious answer is no. There isn't a single policeman or court judge in the world who would take pity on me for what happened, so why even try?

There is, however, an alternative option. It's surprising I didn't think of it before, but if I could make sure Jax is out of reach at the end of these seven days, what could Megan really do to me? Report me to the police? Sure, but I'll rat her out as well, and the police will arrest her before she can

The Guest Bedroom

get anywhere near my son. All I have to do is find somewhere for him to go.

Unfortunately, there's only one place. It hurts to even think about it.

But there's no other choice.

Not if I want to keep my son safe.

It took two long hours to drive to her house, and Jax cried the whole way. The only good thing about this is that he's exhausted himself and is asleep when we arrive. Not that my mother cares about him at all, but at least now she'll have good reason not to engage him.

I have him in the detached car seat by my feet when I ring the doorbell. The living room curtains twitch while I stand there awkwardly, not having rehearsed my speech even a little bit. The house is a big old thing that cost her very little before she did it up and is now worth a fortune. No doubt she'll assume I'm here for some of that money, and that's a part of the problem: she always insisted how great a mother she was simply because there's a large inheritance waiting for me, but what she doesn't understand is that I'd happily give up every last penny if it means having a mother for once.

Somehow, I doubt she'll ever understand.

A latch behind the door rattles, and then it opens. My mother – the 'old bag' as Megan so aptly put it – stands before me in an old-fashioned, floral cotton dress that makes her look like a farmer's wife. Her cheekbones protrude from her wrinkly skin, and her cloudy blue eyes study me with nothing but suspicion.

'I need help,' I tell her bluntly.

'There's no room for you in my house,' she says. 'You'll have to—'

'That's not the kind of help I need. Can we talk?'

Once more, I'm assessed as a potential threat. It takes about thirty seconds for her to decide I'm not a worthless piece of crap. Then she widens the gap in the door and turns her back on me. I pick up the baby seat and carry Jax inside, careful not to knock it on anything.

Closing the front door behind me, I follow Mum through to the dining room, where it reeks with overpowering lavender and the old-fashioned furniture is the only distraction from the ugly-as-hell striped wallpaper. The whole room is hideously outdated but still looks new. Like it was designed forty years ago but only decorated today.

The Guest Bedroom

'What do you need?' Mum asks, getting straight to the point as she sits at the oak dining table. The only sounds in this room are her rough breathing and the loud ticking of the nearby clock – a black-and-white cat with googly eyes and a swinging tail.

I set Jax's seat on the table and perch on the edge of a dining room chair, not wanting to lean against the hard wooden back. There's no point in messing around, so I cut the crap and simply ask for what I need.

'There's trouble,' I say. 'At home. I was wondering if you could watch Jax.'

Mum's eyes widen as she shakes her head. 'No. I couldn't... I have a busy day.'

'Relax, I don't need you to do it today. Maybe in about three days' time.'

'But I'm busy then, also.'

'Mum.' I sigh. 'We both know you don't have a single event planned for the rest of your life. Now will you please just do me a favour and watch your grandson for a few days?'

'A few days?'

'Yes. It's really important.'

'What could possibly be so important?'

An exasperated breath huffs out of me. I sound

like a dragon priming for a blast of fire. 'That's actually a secret, which is a part of the problem. But the long story short is that he might be in danger. We might *all* be in danger, given the circumstances.'

'Will you try to be a little less cryptic?'

'Not really. It's too complicated.'

Mum rubs her eyes as if she's been up for days without a minute of sleep, then reaches for her glasses. Her liver-spotted hands shake as she slides them on to her face and then pushes herself out of the chair. It's not until now that I realise just how much she resembles a skeleton. Then, without so much as glancing at her grandson, she leaves the room.

I wait it out for a minute, hoping she'll soon return with a pot of tea or even just a glass of water to refresh me from my long drive. When the beam of sunlight pouring in through the window has shifted a couple of inches, I give up and go through to the kitchen, leaving Jax asleep in the dining room but keeping an eye on him from the doorway.

That's when I see my mother. Drinking wine straight from the bottle. Again.

I snatch it right out of her hands. She protests, but I pour it straight down the sink while feeling

The Guest Bedroom

sick at the idea of leaving a six-month-old in this woman's hands. I wouldn't ask if I weren't desperate, however, but the least I can do is wash her problem down the plughole.

'That bottle costs two thousand pounds,' she says moodily.

'And now it's worth nothing. Look, I need your help.'

'I already told you—'

'Okay, *Jax* needs your help. Can you step up?'

'Well, I don't know...'

'I'm not asking for much.' I approach her, paying no mind to the additional wine bottles sitting in the cabinet behind her. Normally, I would be more judgemental, but right now all I'm concerned about is getting some childcare for my son. Then maybe – just maybe – I can get through the whole Megan situation without the possibility of kidnapping. 'Please, Mum.'

She shakes her head and looks down. That's usually a telltale sign that she's about to say no, but she must see the desperation in my eyes when she meets my gaze. I must be desperate if I'm coming to her, that look says, and perhaps that triggers her understanding of my situation, even if she doesn't know the smallest fraction of the story.

'Will you stay for dinner?' she asks, changing the subject.

'Mum...'

'Stay for dinner. Tell me why you need help, then I'll consider doing it.'

There's nothing I hate more than spending time with this woman. She never did care about me, and over the years I've learned to distance myself. Finding the humility to come back now was not easy, and the only thing that's going to change is it will be even harder.

Because not only do I have to tell her my story.

But she can't cook to save her life.

As soon as I've washed the dishes, I return to the living room where Mum is sitting with Jax. She looks so stiff and awkward, holding her grandson at arm's length as if a single bite from him would turn her into a zombie. Jax, on the other hand, is just staring at her with wandering eyes while he tries to figure out whether or not he likes her.

'You'll do just fine,' I say after clearing my throat. 'He likes you.'

'You can't possibly know that,' she tells me.

I just shrug and join her on the sofa. The

The Guest Bedroom

favour I've asked for goes unspoken, and I know better than to push. My mother will come around when she's good and ready. Meanwhile, I have to sit here anxiously awaiting her decision.

It has to be the only thing I've asked for her since becoming an adult. She wasn't there for my wedding, and nor did she make it to the hospital when Jax was born. In fact, this is only the second time she's met him, which makes it the first time she's *held* him. You might think it's nuts for me to trust a woman like that but, when you get this desperate, there's not a whole lot you can do to keep your kid safe.

Before it starts getting dark, I yawn and get up. Jax is ready to sleep, so tonight is going to be an absolute nightmare while his body clock adjusts. I hope it's going to be worth it, but my mother leads me out to the doorstep without bringing up the one thing I asked her for. When she says goodbye, it suddenly becomes clear that this is my responsibility.

'Are you going to help me?' I ask in a breath.

Almost without hesitation, Mum shakes her head. 'I can't.'

My heart starts racing as if I've been struck by lightning. 'Why not?'

'Having a child was your decision, not mine.'

'I'm not asking you to adopt him. You'd just have to watch him for a few days.'

'And I'm telling you no. I've done my share of raising a child, and I'm done with it.'

Not going to lie, that one hurt. I stand there on her doorstep for a while, tricking myself into thinking her last comment was just a joke and that she'll suddenly turn around and accept the request. Only, the longer I wait, the more likely it seems that she's serious. I stare at her, and she stares back, and that's when I know for certain.

My mother has no intention of helping me. She won't keep Jax safe while I handle the situation, which means Megan can easily get to him. If I have to live with the knowledge that she could have stopped that from happening and refused for no good reason at all, then what I'm thinking as we head back to the car is justified.

I'll probably never see this woman again.

Chapter 13
Becca

It's almost Jax's bedtime when I pull up on the drive. My focus should be drawn towards that, but instead my eyes are glued to the upstairs bedroom window. The light is on up there, which strikes me as strange because Jordan hates using the room for anything but sleeping and getting dressed. Well, there is one other thing involving the bed, but it couldn't be that...

Could it?

Trying not to overthink it, I kill the engine and work on getting Jax out of the car. This is usually the part where Jordan comes rushing out to help me, but maybe he didn't hear me pull up. It's no big deal – I can do this by myself, even if my son is getting a bit heavier to haul out of the car. I'm just glad he hasn't fallen asleep early and broken his entire routine.

Holding him closely in my arms, I trudge up the drive and wrestle to get the door open. As soon as I'm inside, Jax starts wriggling to get free. I just about manage to set him on his tummy before I lose my grip, then shut the door and spin around.

It's hard to explain what happens next. People talk about how they freeze on the spot, but it never truly feels possible. I know that feeling now, as Megan comes down the stairs with a satisfied grin on her face, her hair ruffled and her cheeks red. It's like she's been at some frantic activity, which fills me with horror as I remember the bedroom light was on.

'Welcome home,' she says with a smirk, then disappears into the next room.

I'm stunned, my feet like breeze blocks while my heart flutters and hurts. Jordan appears at the top of the stairs next, looking up from his phone and beaming when he sees we've returned. It's so hard to process – one of them looked guilty as hell, while the other looks perfectly innocent. I don't like to get paranoid, and I certainly don't want to jump to any conclusions, but any rational woman might have the same hot flush of jealousy I have.

The Guest Bedroom

Jordan tucks his phone away and comes downstairs to cuddle Jax. Not before kissing me on the cheek, however. I can't help but wonder, were these lips just on Megan? Am I looking too far into such a simple thing, or do I have every right to be suspicious?

Time will tell.

As it turns out, I simply can't wait for time to pass.

My every thought is tainted with paranoia and jealousy. Each time I close my eyes, I see Megan's polished nails all over my husband. I picture that sly face, a disgusting grin spreading across her lips as she mounts Jordan and takes everything from me. It might not even be something she wants, but that wouldn't stop her from doing it. If I know Megan at all, this is something she would do just to make life more difficult for me.

But would Jordan do it?

I never thought of him as a cheater. There was one incident a few years ago that I dismissed as petty jealousy at the time, but this evening's situation has given me cause to think twice. We were at a wedding reception, having a great time and drinking a lot. A woman needed to pass by, so she tapped Jordan on the shoulder and smiled at him as she threaded herself between the crowd. Jordan, dazzled by her beauty, tried to say something to her. Only an awkward jumble of words came out, laced with a schoolboy-like chuckle. I should have known at the time that he was smitten, but I've spent this whole time convincing myself it wasn't a red flag.

Does that make me a fool?

Jordan is taking care of Jax now, putting him to bed just to give me a short break. I'm desperately trying not to overthink it, but Megan keeps strolling through the house and making comments about how her hips hurt. Is she trying to tell me something? Is she trying to taunt me, or tease me into thinking what I already know in my heart could be true?

There's only one way to find out.

I head upstairs in search of evidence. Jordan is still in the nursery. His low voice a grumble through the door as he reads our son a bedtime story. It gives me an opportunity to go into our bedroom and find something. What, exactly?

Who knows?

I start with the bed, where the duvet is on

The Guest Bedroom

neatly but not the way I left it. Jordan doesn't tuck the sides in like I do, so I know for an absolute fact that he's messed up the bed and then had to remake it. Naturally, my heart sinks at this revelation, but it's not enough. There has to be more – something undeniably telling.

The en-suite bathroom bin is my next destination, where I quickly drop to my knees and start rummaging through its contents. There's some tissue, an ungodly amount of dental floss, but no sign of what I'm looking for – a used condom. That could mean anything though... right? Megan already told me she can't conceive, so would she even see any point in using protection? One can only imagine she has some sort of Pokémon-like mentality towards sexually transmitted infections (gotta catch 'em all), and Jordan should know better.

So, then... where's the evidence?

It's all I can think about, and I'm going spare. Sitting right here on the bathroom floor, tears are starting to sting my tired eyes. My husband and I have gone through some rough times just like any couple, but I never truly thought he was capable of cheating on me. Now, I'm not so sure. I think back again to that incident at the wedding reception. A flurry of memories comes to me like a time-lapse video, retracing my steps through our whole marriage and thinking of every time he ever looked at another woman. Every time he left the room to check his phone. It might have been innocent, but it might have been sinister.

As for Megan? There's not a single doubt in my mind that she would do this to me. She's always been known for sinking her claws into what she wants and never letting go. I feel sick just thinking about it – that she would sleep with Jordan just to get at me. As if grabbing me by the throat wasn't enough. As if taking my son away from me isn't recompense enough for whatever she *thinks* I've done wrong. Knowing her, she probably isn't even angry at me for anything in particular. It's no secret that she's a nasty bitch.

And now, maybe, she's a homewrecker, too.

THIS IS where I'm supposed to be: lying on Jordan's bare chest and feeling the soothing rhythm of his heartbeat. The duvet is covering us up to our waists, but it's folded back because the bedroom is a little warmer than we're comfortable with. At least that's what I told him. The truth is, it no

The Guest Bedroom

longer feels like *my* duvet. It smells of Megan without actually smelling of Megan. The cotton suddenly feels old, like I picked it up from a used-goods marketplace and it's stained with the history of past lovers. I never thought my own bed would feel this way.

I'm drawing circles around my husband's chest, fluffing back his thick hair and watching it fall back on to his ribs. I want to explore his body as if it's brand new to me, but this is likely just my brain's way of telling me to reclaim what's rightfully mine. I want to kiss him, touch him in places he likes to be touched, but he hasn't showered since *maybe* sleeping with Megan. He, like our duvet, now feels like used goods to me.

Of course, I can spend all night wondering what really happened between the two of them. I've seen it in TV dramas, where an annoying-as-hell character spends too much time mulling over something that can easily be resolved by simply asking. It won't go down well, but it wouldn't be right to lie here wondering what the truth is without having the basic respect to actually *ask* the man I love. The man who has given me everything.

'Did you have sex with Megan?' I blurt out like it's nothing – as if I'm simply asking whether he would like a cup of coffee or a snack. The silence that follows drags on for too long, and now my head is swimming with even more insane theories.

'What? No,' he says at long last, then sits up and shrugs me off. 'Why would you ask that?'

The duvet pulls away from me as he gains some distance, sitting up against the headboard while he studies me. I gather the bedding up and cover myself, suddenly cold. In fact, it seems like the temperature in the whole room has dropped ten degrees.

'Everything just felt wrong when I got in the door,' I say.

'When? Tonight?'

'Yeah.'

'I don't understand.'

'It's just that you and Megan came down the stairs one after the other. She knows I don't want her going up there, and she betrayed my wishes. Then she gave me this look that... is hard to explain. But it's telling, and it made me wonder.'

Jordan shakes his head in disbelief. 'She was upstairs because she heard me scream.'

'You screamed? Why?'

'Because I stubbed my toe on the corner of the bed.'

The Guest Bedroom

'Why were you in bed?'

'I wanted to nap. It's been a long day.'

'But her cheeks were red.'

'So? It's hot up here. You know that.'

The whole thing seems off. Jordan rarely naps, if ever. Although it would explain why the bed was a mess, I still hate the idea that Megan was up here, standing in our bedroom. Maybe more than that. Maybe I'll never know.

'You know what?' Jordan says, scooting away by a few inches as if he can't bear to have me touch him any more. 'I'm getting tired of all this. You've not been the same since Megan arrived. You used to be happy, easy-going, and fun. The woman I married seems to have been left in last week, and now I'm talking with a highly strung, negative, paranoid...'

Somehow, he manages to stop himself. I watch him in the silence of the dimly lit room, asking myself over and over what the next word was going to be. My heart is aflutter, slowly cracking as it starts to break. My own husband is angry at me – perhaps even despises me. What does this mean for us moving forward? I'm pushing him away, right? So... who am I pushing him towards? It's a horrible way to think, but I can't help it.

'I'm sorry,' I say sincerely. 'It just brings up a lot of emotions.'

'Then get rid of her.'

'It's not that simple.'

'No, nothing seems to be at the moment.'

'What's that supposed to mean?'

'Nothing. Listen.' Jordan leans forward and cups my hand in his. It's warm. Familiar. His eyes lock on to mine, but not in the way a lover's would. It could just be me, but this feels more like a performance. 'Nothing happened between Megan and I. Even if we weren't married, she's not my type. I love *you*. Can you please stop acting crazy and put this behind you? You've not got a single thing to worry about. I promise.'

I want to believe him – I really do. But I've heard words like this before. Not from Jordan, to his credit, but from past lovers who at the time seemed just as loyal and trustworthy as he now does. But I'm losing him. I can feel it. That's why I nod, tell him I'm sorry, then turn off the light and try to let him spoon me. He does, which feels nice, but it doesn't feel the same as it used to. I'm starting to worry I've upset him.

But it's not the only thing I'm worried about.

Before I turn off the light, I take a quick glance

The Guest Bedroom

at his foot. There is no mark on his toe, so there's no proof that he stubbed it. Does it mean for sure that he's lying to me? No, not really, but it certainly doesn't stand as evidence of his story either. All it does is leave me feeling as suspicious as I've felt all day.

In short, nothing has changed.

I'm still angry, bitter, and jealous.

Chapter 14
Jordan

WELL, that was a bloody nightmare.

For the record, I really did not have sex with Megan. It may have come pretty close, but I'll get to that when my anger has simmered a little. Frankly, I'm growing sick and tired of Becca's behaviour. I was willing to overlook a lot of it, even let her do her thing without me asking any questions, but now she's accusing me of doing things I simply did not do...

Yet?

Don't ask. The point is, I can't sleep. Somehow, Becca has managed to drift off in my arms. She's lightly dozing now, her soft little snuffles making her sound like a hedgehog. I actually envy her ability to sleep. It's like she's caused her trouble and can now rest safe and sound. Meanwhile, I'm tossing and turning like I'm cursed with insomnia.

Why can't this just be over? Why can't we be rid of Megan already? I'm dying for my wife to return to normal, to remove the temptation of adultery, and then resume our perfect family life as it was always supposed to be. This whole thing is exhausting.

I'm exhausted.

But at least there's one thing keeping me happy. The one thing I truly cannot live without. I love the way he looks at me each morning. I love the way my heart breaks when I have to say goodbye on my way out to work. He always looks disheartened and, although it sounds selfish, it's nice to feel like someone misses me. That's the stuff that keeps me going all day. The thing that makes me want to come home. Because no matter how bad life gets.

I'll always have Jax.

It's a late start for me and, given that I barely slept at all, it would have been great to sleep in just for an hour or two. Unfortunately, Jax is screaming the house down. Teething again, probably. Becca leaps out of bed and assures me I can relax a little before work, but our son's wailing could wake the dead. I might as well get up.

Becca has settled him a little by the time I'm downstairs. I kiss her good morning in an attempt to wipe the slate clean, then play with Jax until he's got some food in his stomach. We're still giving him porridge, and he loves it so much that nothing else seems to exist until his bowl is clear and he's asking for more with some sign language we've been trying to instil. He's such a good kid. Not deserving of any of this house's drama.

The tension only thickens when Megan wakes up, strolling into the kitchen while yawning. I pretend not to notice that she's wearing the same nightie – long and baggy and far more revealing than is appropriate. Becca glances at her then looks to me, almost as if to catch my reaction. It won't work – I'm too good at hiding my feelings. Anyway, it will only make things worse after last night's accusations.

I really am innocent, you know. So I lied a little, as there was no stubbing of the toe or Megan checking in on me to make sure I wasn't hurt.

The Guest Bedroom

What really happened is that I was catching a quick nap on the bed and then woke up to her sitting beside me. It freaked me out, of course, but she played it off like it was nothing.

'You look cute when you're sleeping,' she said.

Still not entirely sure if I was dreaming, I sat up, rubbed my eyes with the heels of my hands, then stared at her (goddamn beautiful) smiling lips. I'd be lying if I said having her next to me wasn't arousing, but I told you before that I'm loyal. That part was not a lie.

'Shouldn't we go downstairs?' I asked, my voice cracking like I was a schoolboy.

'Not necessarily. It could be more fun up here.'

'That's not really appropriate.'

'Why not? Becca isn't here.'

Before I could even begin to think about how to respond to that, her hand snaked over my leg. For some reason, I didn't stop her, but when she got too close to the place where only my wife (and maybe my doctor) should touch me, I had to back away. With an awkward erection that was too hard to hide, I might add. Megan saw it, bit her lip, and raised her eyebrows. Almost like she'd rehearsed it.

'Well, well,' she said. 'You're more into this than you're admitting.'

Once again, I quietly stood there and watched her get up to leave. Then I threw on some jeans and followed her out of the room to make sure she'd go, then reached for my phone to contact Becca. Just as I started to dial her number, I spotted her in the downstairs hallway, watching my every move. Had she overheard what happened?

I hoped not.

Becca has expressed her suspicions, and I tried to talk her down. Now that Megan is nearby, I have to pay full attention to my wife just so she doesn't get any more ideas. Not a single word is spoken between the three of us as we each sort out our breakfast and eat up.

It is getting a little ridiculous. Becca is obviously unhappy with Megan being here, so why the hell isn't she doing something about it? There has to be more going on than first appears, but I'm not ready to press. It would look too much like I'm deflecting – spinning the attention on to her in a desperate attempt to prove my own innocence.

But I'm not technically innocent, am I?

Megan knows this, and she's teasing me with multiple glances across the kitchen. I'm trying not to pay attention, but you can be sure something is stirring in my loins again. I'm almost proud of my

The Guest Bedroom

ability to resist, because right now nothing would please me more than to tear her clothes off and give her everything those stunning eyes are begging me for.

But I must be good.

For our family's sake.

Chapter 15
Becca

THIS MORNING COMES with its own nightmare.

After Jordan somehow magically got me to sleep (he sometimes does that by stroking my back or simply cuddling into me), I was out like a light for a good few hours. There are no dreams, no vicious repeat of awful memories or intrusive fears sticking around to haunt me. It's like I'm dead – completely free of all worry or concern.

Until I hear the scream.

Jax's shrieking blasts through the baby monitor. I roll over and look up with a stiff neck, one eye slowly blinking open and the other not opening at all. My son is rolling around in his cot, unable to remain settled as something bothers him. For a moment, I wonder if Megan is in the room with

The Guest Bedroom

him, but then I quickly remember he could simply be teething.

'I've got this one,' I tell Jordan as he starts to stir.

Just like that, my sleep is over and I'm tending to our little one's needs while early-morning grog starts making me sick. I get him changed, take him downstairs, then try my best to entertain him while preparing his food. It's easy enough this morning: fruit slices and some porridge. Stuff that's not so hard on the teeth.

There's also no sign of the Devil. The door to the guest bedroom is shut, so at least one person has managed to sleep through all the screaming. I have half a mind to go in there and wake her up just to give her a taste of what she *thinks* she'll be living with in a few days. That's when the dizzying reminder hits me.

There are just three days to go.

A shuddering sigh rattles out of me, and I start playing with Jax. How the hell did I find myself in this situation? My anxiety is soaring these past few days, and it wasn't made any better by having to deal with my mother. There's a reason we don't talk much these days, but I honestly thought she would be there for me when it could mean never seeing my son again. Not that she knows the full circumstances – how could she?

My secret is still… well, a secret.

For now.

I really feel like I'm losing my mind, especially after coming home to find Megan returning from my bedroom. My personal space. All in all, it was the worst day since she first came to Collingwood, which is saying something. As I hear Jordan's footsteps creaking through the upstairs floorboards, I'm trying to convince myself that it will only get better. But with each passing minute the simple, horrifying fact keeps circling back around to make me sick with worry.

Just three days to go.

JORDAN COMES DOWNSTAIRS JUST in time to keep me from my own thoughts. People speak of the seven-year itch, where relationships break down due to boredom and frustration with their partners, but I'm not feeling it. If anything, I feel closer to my husband than ever before. Although that could be the impending doom speaking.

He's so good with Jax, taking the stress off my hands and entertaining him so I can enjoy a cup of

The Guest Bedroom

coffee. I love watching the two of them play together, but the fact it may be one of the final times just makes me want to throw up. Once again, the terrible idea of confessing my sins crosses my mind, and then I remember it's just one of the two evils.

Nobody wins either way.

Except for Megan.

Speaking of, the guest bedroom door has just clicked open. My blood pressure elevates as soon as I hear it, and Jordan's head turns. Megan then makes an appearance, wearing basically nothing and swinging her hips to grab my husband's attention. It doesn't work, but I truly believe that's just because he's on his best behaviour.

To tell the truth, I'm still slightly suspicious of those two.

'How did you sleep?' he asks her while looking at me as if to say it's too quiet in here.

'Just fine, thank you.' Megan pours herself a glass of water from the filter and downs it, droplets spilling on to her plain white nightie. 'The mattress is a little firm though. My back is killing me. Could really use a good rub down.'

A what?

I can barely believe my ears. Actually, I would

think I misheard her, but the way she's looking over her glass at my husband tells me I heard correctly. I turn to Jordan, whose face has turned so red it looks like he's been slapped. This feeling coursing through me... it shouldn't be anger towards him, but it is.

'Maybe we can help,' he says, saving the situation. 'There's a good chiropractor in town.'

'What, your hands aren't any good?'

'Excuse me?' I but in, taking a step forward to mark my territory.

Megan drops the glass. It shatters and explodes into a hundred tiny sparkling pieces. Jax screams at the top of his lungs. Jordan picks him up and shushes him for comfort. It should be a distraction to me, but white-hot fury is rushing through me.

'That's my husband you're speaking to, so have some respect.'

'What? I didn't mean—'

'Come on, you knew exactly what you were saying.'

'No, I meant if either of you had experience with...' Megan lowers her head and presses her hands to her ears. It's as if she's a child, trying so desperately to deny there's a monster in her room if she can only block out all sight and sound of it. But

The Guest Bedroom

despite this little show of pity she's putting on, there's only one monster here.

It's her.

Jax is still crying the house down. My hands are still clenched into fists, my nails starting to pierce the skin of my palms. I turn to Jordan, seeking advice with nothing but my eyes, but he's bumping Jax up and down while shushing, somehow able to work in a shrug. It's true that he doesn't know just how evil this woman can be, but surely he can't be completely clueless? I mean, he's a cop for crying out loud.

'It's not my fault.' Megan's voice cracks, and 'crocodile tears' springs to mind. When I wheel back around to watch her, the waterworks have already been turned on. 'I'm so sorry if I upset anyone. Jordan, I didn't mean to make your son cry. I wasn't insinuating... you shouldn't... please don't hurt me, Becca. I'm so sorry!'

With that, she storms out of the room with a great, pitiful sob. If I were a director, I'd be yelling 'cut' right now just to reset the scene. It was so sickeningly fake, I honestly can't believe that just happened. All I do is watch her go back into the guest bedroom, slamming the door behind her with one final, feel-sorry-for-me grunt.

'A little over the top, wasn't it?' Jordan says, Jax finally settling in his arms.

'Just a little.' I roll my eyes. 'Can you believe that woman?'

'Her? I meant you.'

'*Me?*'

My mouth gapes open as I stare in wonder. Jordan shakes his head, practically drowning me in shame since the two of them have just made me believe I did something wrong. My only intention was to protect my man from the evil clutches of that maniacal cow, and now that same man is leaving the room with our son in his arms and a big mess on the kitchen floor. It's hard to say exactly what I'm feeling right now, but it's an awful race between anger, humiliation, and betrayal.

I just don't know which.

I SHOULD HAVE my head in my hands just like Megan did, but I'm finally at breaking point. There's no way I'm going to put up with this any longer, so I do what any half-intelligent being would do and set my phone to record, then storm right into the guest bedroom and shut the door behind me. *Hard.*

The Guest Bedroom

Megan sits up from the bed, her false tears gone and replaced with a furious, creased forehead. 'Hey!' she shouts, getting only halfway up before she registers my own anger. Then she hesitates, if only for a second while she recalibrates.

'You're starting to piss me off,' I spit, pointing a finger right at her like a sword. 'You think you can just waltz right into my home, make your threats, flirt with my husband, then play the victim? You can't. Especially after what *you* did all those years ago.'

Just like that, Megan's frown carves into a smile. 'Turn the recorder off, Becca.'

'What?'

'Don't play dumb. If you want to talk, show me your phone first.'

'I'm not...'

There's no use denying it. I suppose if anyone would know all the little tricks to try to gain leverage, it would be her. After a long and fed-up exhale, I reach into my pocket, turn off the recorder, then turn the screen towards her. 'Satisfied?'

Megan studies it, then nods and passes me. She opens the door, peers outside, then shuts it again and leans back against the heavy wood. When she speaks, her voice is low. Almost a whisper. 'What exactly was your goal here?'

'To make you back the hell off.'

'And you thought that would work?'

'It absolutely will.'

'Do I need to remind you what's at stake here?'

She really doesn't. Jax's safety is on my mind on a minute-to-minute basis, and the thought of losing him is still making me ill. But the helpless feeling it causes? I'm so tired of it. I'm like a fly in a spider's web. My life is almost over, no matter how hard I struggle.

'As if taking my baby isn't enough,' I say carefully, licking my dry lips, 'you want to take my husband away, too? Is there no end to your lunacy?'

'Oh, relax, it was just a bit of flirting.'

'In the kitchen, yes, but what about upstairs?'

Megan cocks her head. 'Huh?'

'Now who's playing dumb?' I sigh. 'Did you or did you not sleep with Jordan?'

'Are you insane?'

'No more than you are. Yes or no?'

'Of course not.'

'And you expect me to believe you?'

'If you weren't going to believe me then why ask?' Megan brushes her hair back with her fingers, then hugs her own chest and steps towards me. Her eyes are lowered at first, but she looks up at me like a grinning menace. 'Sweetheart, he's not my type. Even if he were – and let's say I screw his brains out – I'll be more than happy to let you know about it. There's not exactly a lot you can do about it, is there? Think about it.'

Now I feel *really* sick. Mostly because of the probability of this happening. Although I hate to admit it, she's absolutely right. Sleeping with my man would be a power play for her – a victory that she would scream from the rooftops just to make sure I know my place.

'I want you to stay away,' I say bravely, trying to put my foot down. 'If Jordan walks into the room, you walk out. If he asks you a question, one-word answer him and then go about your day. All this drama is distracting me from the big decision you're forcing me to make, so I need you to be a little lenient and—'

'Becca.' Megan snaps out a hand and clamps it on my shoulder. 'I *am* being lenient. I gave you a week, didn't I? That's out of respect for our friendship. And make no mistake, if I want to ride your husband like Seabiscuit then that's exactly what I'll do. Now, are you going to get off my back, or do you need reminding of who's in charge?'

The twinkle in her eyes matches the evil curvature of her lips. I want to smack her – to hurt her like I've never hurt anyone before – but she'll only hit me back and take what she wants. It suddenly occurs to me that the only way to win a fight with her is to kill her, and that's something I just don't have in me. In short, she was right in what she said the other day.

She owns me.

Chapter 16
Becca

THE REST of the day goes by as normal, except I'm livid. My mind wanders as I play with Jax. I scrub too hard when cleaning the windows. Somehow, I even manage to smash a china plate while washing the dishes, my anger and frustration sitting at the helm of my actions.

It's not fair. My life started kind of poorly, from neglectful parents to a lot of bullying in school which probably contributed to my sensitivity when it comes to feeling pressured and targeted. I always thought things would turn around – that I would marry the perfect man and have the perfect life – and they really did. But now it's being taken away from me. I'm not religious but, if I were, I'd imagine God is handing me a break and then pulling it away at the last second just to mess with me. It's a good thing I don't believe in Him.

But it means I have nobody to blame.

Nobody except myself.

Megan is moving through the house now. I'm standing on the back patio while Jax crawls across the tiles towards the grass. The spring air is cool and refreshing, but the real chill comes from knowing that monster is in my house. It's awful, but I'm starting to fantasise about walking in there and striking her around the head. It would solve all my problems, but it would do a number on my conscience. That's a price I can't afford to pay.

As the day goes on, she and I bump into each other a few times. She starts making herself at home, treating herself to our food and wandering around, even upstairs where I told her not to go. There's no telling what she's doing up there, but it's more than likely she's just exercising her control over me. There's nothing I can do about it either.

The nightmare ends when Jordan returns home from work. As usual, he takes Jax out of my hands, then recognises the stress in my expression. I tell him I'm okay, but then he demands I go upstairs and take an hour or so out. It doesn't take much to convince me, and before I know it the

The Guest Bedroom

steaming shower water is cleansing my skin. I can practically feel my problems washing away and, for once in a long time, my woes seem to be lessened.

Until I go back downstairs.

The first thing I see is Jordan looking over something. He doesn't turn when I say his name – his attention is completely consumed by whatever he's looking at. My heart racing, I make my way towards him, past Jax in his high chair, and start sweating when I see what he's holding. My eyes roam up to his face, where pain and confusion rest as one.

'What is this?' he asks.

'That's... um...'

There's no point in lying, but I can't exactly explain it either. All I can think about is that now it's so obvious why Megan was messing around upstairs. She went through my things. She found the newspaper clippings and, for whatever reason, she left them in the kitchen.

Where my husband can see them.

'Where did these come from?' he presses.

'They're mine.'

'Why do you have them?'

I swallow a dry lump just as it forms in my throat, then blow out a ragged breath. Jordan stares at me, his eyes challenging. Is this how criminals feel when he interrogates them? Is this what the scum of Collingwood go through when he pierces them with that fierce glare? It's so disarming, borderline terrifying, and I feel like a little girl being scorned. It makes me want to tell him everything, but the truth is that I can't. No matter how much I want to be honest with the man I love – the man I *married* – he's asking questions I simply cannot answer.

And it's breaking both our hearts.

Megan appears at just the right moment, that sadistic grin plastered on her face. She's caused a rift between my husband and me, and she knows it. She's *enjoying* it. I've never felt so much hate for another human being as I do right now. Why does she have to do this to me? Is taking my child away not enough? Is holding my life hostage not going to satisfy her?

She moves to the kitchen table and sits down, watching. Jordan doesn't seem to notice she's entered the room, but I feel her eyes all over me. They're toxic, poisonous. Like a venomous snake, always watching... and waiting to strike.

The Guest Bedroom

'Are you going to answer me?' Jordan demands. There's no love in his voice. Just utter distrust, and it only grows harsher when I don't respond to him. 'Becca, I would like to know why you have newspaper clippings of an incident that happened over fifteen years ago. In your home town, no less. What's going on? Talk to me.'

I have to consider every word that comes out of my mouth. Jordan is a police officer, which means he has resources. I don't want to lie to him, but if I give him an inch then he'll pull on that thread and quickly unravel the whole yarn. That would be disastrous to our marriage and, ultimately, to our family.

All I can do is deny it.

'They're not mine,' I say, still feeling Megan's eyes on me. 'Or... maybe they are, but I honestly don't know why they're here. I must have found them interesting and put them in a box once upon a time. Obviously, I forgot about them because they mean nothing to me.'

'Right? So why are they here now?'

'You mean...' I'm stalling, and it's pathetic.

'Why did you leave them out for me? I'm so confused.'

'I didn't leave them out.'

'You must have!'

At the authoritative snap of his voice, Megan's chair glides back. It screeches against the kitchen tiles as she rushes forward in the blink of an eye, her hands up in a semi-defensive position. 'They're mine,' she says. 'That's why Becca doesn't remember them.'

Jordan studies her suspiciously. 'They're yours?'

'Yes, the woman in the incident was a friend of mine, and I keep these clippings with me at all times. It's kind of a reminder of my old life. A comfort thing, really.'

'I don't believe you.'

Megan frowns. 'Why not?'

'Because of how Becca reacted.'

'I'm sorry,' I say, crossing my arms and taking a step back. 'Honestly, it just felt like I was being put under the spotlight. For all I knew, the clippings really were mine and, like I said, I must have just forgotten about them.'

'And Megan?' he pivots. 'You waited this long to speak up?'

'I didn't want to interrupt you. It's not really my business.'

Jordan sighs in the way he only ever does

The Guest Bedroom

under extreme stress. He's having trouble believing this, but he doesn't exactly have much of a choice. The lie is out there – Megan saw to that – and now I'm just wondering why she did that. What exactly is her game? Other than to cause friction, I suppose. That's all she was ever good for.

'You two need to get your act together. If nothing else, get your lies straight.'

Without another word, Jordan drops the clippings on the kitchen counter and storms out, taking Jax in his arms as he passes. I'm left fuming at Megan but unsure of what to say. It even takes her a few seconds to drop the sorrowful mask and return to her usual sneer.

'What the hell was all that about?' I ask.

'Just having a little fun.'

'That fun almost dropped me in it.'

'Exactly. That's what makes it so fun.' Megan scoops up the clippings and raises them. 'Mind if I keep these?' she asks, but she doesn't wait for an answer before leaving the kitchen.

That's my clippings gone, a close call made, and yet another problem between me and my family. I'm not sure how much longer I can do this. Each day is getting harder, and even if Megan wasn't constantly creating more drama, I'd still be on edge because of the ticking time bomb above my head. I'm anxiously awaiting the explosive moment when my entire life blows up in my face, and even after all this time I still don't know what to do.

Everything is falling apart.

Have you ever heard a voice in your dream that feels so real it wakes you up? That's what just happened to me. I was sleeping so peacefully, but Megan whispered in my ear and made me shoot to alertness. It takes a few seconds for me to realise it wasn't real, but by then Jordan is awake and putting a calming hand on my shoulder.

'What's going on with you?' he asks.

The panting subsides. I catch my breath. 'It's not like I can even tell you.'

'Why not?'

'It's complicated.'

'Uncomplicate it.'

I rummage around in the dark to find the bedside lamp, then flood the room with light. We both sit up, my eyes stinging at the harshness of the lamp. I really need to get some energy-saving bulbs in here, but it probably won't matter for too much longer. I'll either be in prison or the gutter, my wrists slashed as an easy alternative to living a life without Jax.

It's every parent's nightmare.

'You need to start communicating a little,' Jordan says. 'I'm your husband. It's my job to hear you out and support you, but I can't do that if you don't talk. Whatever it is that's going on – whatever it is you're hiding – tell me and we'll get through it together.'

I really want to tell him. Of course I do. But given the severity of my secret, it's the worst possible move. No amount of love between a husband and wife can lead a man to forgive what I did. And right now, I'm sitting here in bed knowing that our son is about to be taken away from us, and I can't even say anything to stop that from happening.

Unless...

'Do you trust me?' I ask.

'Honestly? Right now I'm not so sure. You're freaking me out a little.'

That hurts, but it's not surprising. I haven't exactly been upfront with him, and trust is earned. All the same, I sit up and look him in the eye, taking his hand. We hold each other's gaze while I try to think of the right words.

Are there even any right words for this situation?

'What if I told you something bad will happen?' I say.

'Bad, like... how bad?'

'Life-shatteringly awful.'

'Then I'd want to know what it is.'

'What if I can't tell you? Can you at least make me a promise?'

Jordan looks sceptical, his eyebrow raising. 'What promise?'

'If I...' My hand is shaking, but he squeezes it. 'If I ask you not to leave Jax alone with Megan, can you do everything in your power to make sure that doesn't happen?'

'Becca, are we in trouble here?'

'Maybe.'

'Is our son in danger?'

'Maybe.'

'Is Megan a threat to our child? Because if she is—'

'No,' I blurt out. Imagine if he acts on my worries and throws Megan out. What will she do then? How will she react, and what will she do with my big secret? If that was going to happen, I'd rather it be under circumstances I can control. 'Lis-

The Guest Bedroom

ten, I can't tell you what's going on, but I want to. I can't tell you why I'm so scared, but I am. Can you please just promise me you won't leave them alone together? No matter what—'

'Becca, tell me—'

'*Please*, Jordan.'

'Tell me what's—'

'Please!' I scream so loud that Jax stirs through the baby monitor. I burst into tears and Jordan wraps his arms around me. He shushes me and tells me everything will be okay – that he promises he won't let Megan near Jax if neither one of us is around. I rest my cheek against his chest and feel his heart beating. It's full of all the love he has for me.

And now, all the distrust.

Chapter 17
Becca

I want to tell him. He deserves to know. But how can I?

My secret disgusts even me.

Lying in his arms tonight, I somehow manage to drift back to sleep. I listen to his heart, and it's like music to me. Only songs can have this calming effect, and only the memory of that fateful night can upset the rhythm of my own pulse, making me stir until an ungodly hour as the worst day of my life makes an appearance in my head.

It was one of those evenings back in my home town, where the heat was so intense that everyone was wishing for winter. Megan and I were seventeen then, best friends since primary school and not much was likely to change. We'd done everything together, sharing toys, then sharing boys, and now we were like sisters. It's safe to say I loved her with every fibre of my being and, if you asked anyone who saw us together, she loved me right back.

But it wasn't always just the two of us. There was a third friend named Mary-Ann, who went by the name of Mez. Being in the school year below us, she always had trouble squeezing her way between us. I tried to accept her, but Megan was less welcoming. See, Mez was a beautiful girl with a heart of gold, and she easily got all the boys. *All* the boys. Even the ones she didn't want. Even the ones *Megan* wanted.

That was why Megan didn't want her there that night. The train bridge we always used to hang out under had always felt like a retreat. We would drink alcohol, smoke cigarettes, and signal at the trains to use their horns as they blared past, whipping at our hair with hot blasts and making our hearts race. Don't ask me how, but Mez had figured out our little hang-out spot and insisted she come with us that night. Megan didn't like it, of course, but Mike and Josh came with her, and she liked them. It was sort of a package deal.

We did what most dumb teenagers would do;

drank, smoked, kissed, touched, and enjoyed each other's company until the sun rose and we all started feeling a little too fuzzy. Mike managed to score with Megan between the trees, but it was Josh she really wanted. The problem was, Josh was into Mez... and they enjoyed each other right in front of us.

Now, I know what you're thinking. This is all getting a little too school drama, right? Bear with me, because it's about to head in the opposite direction.

Mike left after he got what he wanted. Josh followed, not wanting to get stuck under a train bridge with a bunch of teenage girls who were getting more and more temperamental as the night went on. Before we knew it, it was just the three of us again. We packed up in silence and began to head home in the same direction. Even then, I could feel the awkwardness between us. It was like the boys had come in and ripped the already fragile friendship circle apart.

Nobody said anything as we made our way through the town. It was five o'clock and the sun was rising. The sky was burning a gorgeous orange, hints of blue rising to meet it when the clouds drifted over our town. I began to shiver at long last, which was when Mez slipped off her jacket and put it around me like real gentlemen used to do.

'You might as well kiss her,' Megan said sarcastically. 'You're kissing everyone else.'

Mez looked at me, her face twisted in puzzlement. I shrugged and patted her on the shoulder, then we all continued on. Megan trailed behind, mumbling something under her breath. I think the alcohol was getting to her more than she was letting on. It stayed that way – uncomfortably quiet – until we passed over the top of another train bridge not far from home.

'When will you see Josh again?' Megan asked then.

This time, Mez stopped walking. I could feel the tension burning a hole in our friendship, but it wasn't my place to say anything. Not just yet. Mez, however, had finally had enough of that ridiculous rivalry. She spun around and, without thinking, blurted out her reply.

'Jealousy is an ugly colour on you. In fact, most colours are.'

'What did you just say to me?'

Megan lashed out, lunging forward with her nails primed and ready to scratch. I stepped between them, but I wasn't fast enough. Megan managed to land a scratch on her, to which I reactively pushed Mez out of the way. It was one of those moments that happened so fast that nobody knew exactly what happened until it was too late.

I'd pushed too hard. Mez stumbled back, her foot giving out under an avalanche of dry dirt. She screamed and grasped at thin air as gravity pulled her down the bank. My heart leapt into my throat and I let out a little yelp of horror as my friend fell down the hill. Megan didn't move. Neither did I. We just waited there in the evergrowing silence, listening for Mez to scream up that she was okay – that she had survived the fall and wasn't too badly hurt.

But it never happened.

I DON'T KNOW what came over me. Megan screamed my name as I darted down the bank. Stones rolled out from under me as I ran, dust exploding up into the sunrise. I could see my friend's unmoving body down there, and there was blood – so much blood. I instantly thought of the surrounding woodland and how hard it would be to drag her up. How could we even get her to a hospital? How would we explain this to the police?

The Guest Bedroom

I reached Mez pretty fast, almost tumbling down the bank myself. Her back had hit the railway track, and her temple was coated in crimson. My hands were trembling like leaves in a storm, my body feeling weightless and making me feel sick. I knelt at Mez's side, knowing I had to help but too scared to touch her. I was only vaguely aware of Megan catching up behind me. Less enthusiastically, one might add.

'Mez?' I said in a desperate croak. 'Talk to me. Are you okay?'

But Mez *couldn't* talk. At least not with anything other than her eyes. I'll never forget the way they looked up at me – begging me to run and get her help. Pleading for an explanation as to why I'd done this to her. That was when the tears came, and I told her in a spluttering mess that I'd only been trying to help her. That I hadn't intended to push her, and now she was seriously injured all because of my goddamn stupid reactions.

'She's as good as dead,' Megan said coldly, and for the first time I sensed something of a monster in her. A soulless, emotionless beast who would stop at nothing to get what she wanted. Was that what all this was about? Winning Josh from Mez?

'What did you say?' I snarled.

'You heard me. She's not going to recover from this.'

'Of course she is.'

'I mean, she might, but she'll be paralysed.'

That sickening feeling intensified, and I went on to ignore Megan. It was easier to do when Mez reached for my hand. I could feel her trying to squeeze, but the strength had left her. Now it was just the three of us, hesitating for far too long while the fear prevented me from making a sensible decision. Bear in mind I was essentially a child. They didn't teach kids how to react to real-life situations. That was something that only came with the harsh lessons in life.

This was definitely one of those lessons.

I finally snapped out of my shock and thought to reach for my phone. Back then, we weren't constantly connected to social media and sending pictures every five seconds, so I barely remembered it was there. I let go of Mez's hand – I'll never forget her desperate whimper – and dug into my pocket for the phone. I tried not to look at my bleeding friend as my quivering hand messed up something as simple as dialling for an ambulance. Not that I got that far.

Because Megan had other ideas.

The Guest Bedroom

It happened so fast that I couldn't have stopped it even if I'd been prepared. At first all I saw was a rush of colour, Megan's vibrant blue top whizzed past me. The next thing I knew, she was at Mez's side with a large rock raised high above her head. I tried to stop her – tried to scream – but all that came out was air. That was when the rock came down, a dull, sickening thud striking Mez's skull. Not just once, not twice, but three times. I knew it was over when Mez's hand stopped shaking. Then, with grim finality, Megan dropped the blood-coated rock on to the dirt and stepped back. Neither of us said anything, because what was there to say?

Our friend was dead.

It was both our faults.

TIME CAME AND WENT, but the next train didn't. It gave us a long time to think over every agonising detail of what was going to happen next. Megan tried to tell me this wasn't going to end well if we let this little secret out. Perhaps that was how she convinced me to help her hide the body. How she persuaded me to cover up our friend's murder.

As we dragged her into the bushes, I tried not

to look at her eyes. I couldn't help it. They stared so desperately up at the sky, as if to ask for help that wasn't going to come. Tears stung my eyes, but I persevered until we were all well-hidden, concealed behind trees and foliage. Megan clawed at the dirt with her bare hands to make a grave only a foot or so deep, then started throwing branches and leaves over her body (*oh God, her body!*). All the while, I stood there like an idiot just wishing I could rewind the clock and have Mez back with us.

A little while later, we each looked at the pile of leaves. Megan and I didn't say anything for a long time. I can't tell you what she was thinking, but I was terrified of her from that moment on. Nothing would ever be the same again. *Nothing*.

After all, we had just killed our friend.

'The animals should take care of it over time.'

"It," I scoffed. 'Mez isn't a thing, Megan. She's a person.'

'She was. Now she's food for the wildlife.'

It took every ounce of strength not to slap her but, like I said, she scared the hell out of me. I'd never seen anyone kill a person before, but the way Megan so emotionlessly finished her off made me think of her as something far from human. There was mania in her eyes and bloodlust in her actions. It was like she'd been waiting a long time for this.

We climbed back up the bank and made our way back on to the bridge. There was woodland all around us, and not a single car had passed this entire time. If there was only one thing going right that day, that was it. I remember looking over the side of the bridge and not being able to see the exposed grave we'd just walked away from. It was probably a good thing, seeing as neither of us wanted to go to prison.

So I just stared up the track as the rails began to hiss. The train sounded its horn from far away, and the current picked up to an electrifying spark. Megan grabbed my wrist then – too hard, everything was too hard – and looked me dead in the eye.

'You killed her,' she said. 'She was as good as dead right after you pushed her.'

'That's not... I didn't...'

'You did, Becca. All I did was finish her off.'

My free hand came to my mouth as if to clamp in a cry. It didn't work, because a strange guttural sound exploded from my throat. It was just sinking in that I was a killer. It may not have been deliberate, but I'd killed my friend and helped Megan hide the body. At the time I thought it was to protect me, but now that I'm older I know better.

The train closed the distance. It was nearby now. Megan held my gaze and told me this had to stay a secret. If it ever came out, both of us would go down, but she was going to make my life a living hell if I so much as thought about confessing my sins. Given what she'd done and how easily she'd done it, I firmly believed her threats. Then, as the train tore up the space under us and rattled the bridge, I suddenly realised that life would never be the same again.

We were killers now.

That was our secret.

Chapter 18
Jordan

I'm up multiple times throughout the night. Everything Becca said to me has been playing on a loop, which has kept me awake for obvious reasons. I just can't get my head around why someone would think this is okay. How can you expect a father not to be concerned when his wife is having a freak-out over the stranger in the spare room?

It made the night a long one. For painful stretches, I would stand in the corner of the nursery and just watch my son sleeping. I didn't turn the light on, and I quite enjoyed the dark, but a small part of me wondered if Megan might try to sneak in. But to do what? To hurt him? Take him? She's had plenty of chances to do both and he's been okay so far.

So then, what is my wife so afraid of?

The sun is rising now. Hours of exhaustion are catching up to me, my eyes feeling tight and tired. I have work in a few hours, and somehow I'm expected to perform as if I'm a sensible adult catching a reasonable amount of sleep. But the truth is I haven't been sleeping right ever since Megan arrived. Ever since Becca started acting like… well, like this.

Jax is starting to wriggle. These are the hours where his sleep is more loose and broken. He must sense I'm in the room, because he cranes his neck and looks up in my direction, even with his eyes closed. It's too hard to resist picking him up, so I rest him against my chest and sit in the armchair by the window. I love this little guy – his snoring, his grunts, his laughter. If Megan really is a threat then I need to pay some serious attention to her backstory, and yesterday's incident with the newspaper clippings was nothing short of suspicious.

Nobody – and I mean *nobody* – keeps physical copies of a news story like that unless they have a guilty conscience. That, or something to hide. Either way, I'm no idiot and I intend to get to the bottom of this sinister connection between her and Becca.

The Guest Bedroom

Even if it kills me.

The rest of the house wakes up slowly. Megan is nowhere to be seen while I feed Jax, which is something to be grateful for. Becca sleeps in just a little because I turned off her alarm and the baby monitor to let her catch up on some rest. I worry that fatigue might have something to do with her recent behavioural changes. God, I hate using that expression. It makes it seems as though she's a toddler. Or worse – insane.

When she does eventually join me, she kisses and hugs me. It's not the same as the way she used to do it. It used to be so full of love and promise, but now she just seems vacant. Distracted. I can tell she's on the verge of having a panic attack, but she keeps her thoughts to herself. As selfish as it sounds, that's probably for the best.

'Do you want me to take Jax this morning?' I ask her, noticing her red eyes.

'No, that's okay. You have work.'

'Not until this afternoon.'

'Then go and have some downtime. Read your book or—'

The door to the guest bedroom clicks open

then. Becca stops talking as if she was committing a crime and just got busted. I watch Megan enter the kitchen, fully dressed this time, thank God. Although I must admit, it's harder to find her attractive ever since I became suspicious of her. I'm human and have needs and desires, but that doesn't make me illogical.

'How are we all doing today?' Megan asks as she passes, softly pinching Jax's cheek.

Jax giggles, and Becca takes a reactive but restrained step towards them. Megan shoots her a glare, and then my wife backs off. Whatever is going on between them, I sincerely hope it's resolved soon. I'm losing my patience, hating the drama, and thinking about throwing her out myself seeing as Becca is too scared to do it. I only wonder if that will make things harder for the two of them. I guess we might find out.

'We're fine,' Becca says like they're worst enemies. 'Just about to have breakfast.'

'Oh, good, I'm starving.'

'I was talking about me and my family.'

'Becca,' I say, blown away by her sudden rudeness. Then an idea occurs to me, and it's out of my mouth without giving it too much thought. 'Actually, I was thinking about taking Jax out for a walk. Maybe you two can enjoy some food alone together.'

My wife's eyes widen with alarm. 'No, that's—'

'Not necessary,' Megan finishes.

A soft smile finds its way to my lips. They act like they don't get along, but they're finishing each other's sentences. To tell the truth, I'm absolutely starving, but maybe leaving these two alone might force them to get along and put whatever problems they have behind them. Also, it keeps Jax away from Megan as requested.

'I'm going,' I tell them, 'and that's the end of it.'

They both have faces like slapped arses, but it's not my problem. My only concern is getting my little guy into his buggy and then heading out the door. Nobody says anything when I leave, and Becca doesn't even kiss me, but whatever. I'm merely a mortal man and can only do so much in a situation as bizarre as this. So I continue down the drive and barely make it on to the road before I hear my name carried on the wind.

I stop and turn. It's Megan, hurrying after me with her jacket tucked over her arm. The last thing I want is her company, but it doesn't look like I have any control over what these women do. Nor do I really want to, given how explosive I can get when frustrated.

'Want some company?' Megan asks, smiling as she reaches me.

'Not really.'

'Funny.' She throws her head back with an exaggerated laugh.

It's tempting to just tell her outright that she's better off heading back inside. I have to walk Jax anyway, and the whole purpose of it was to put the two of them together. But before I can protest, her hand snakes around my arm that's extended to the buggy handles, and she's beaming up at me as if she's been in love with me since the day we met.

Who knows? Maybe she has.

'I won't take no for an answer,' she says. 'Come on, show me around town.'

There are a thousand different ways to handle this, but none of them will work. I take a deep breath, frankly extremely concerned about how this is going to play out. Then I take a look back at the house and see Becca in the window, flicking her hand as if to encourage this. Maybe she can't see how close Megan is to me, or maybe she doesn't

The Guest Bedroom

care. Either way, I'm going to take her advice rather than risk annoying two women at once.

It's settled. Megan and I are going for a walk.

Together.

Chapter 19
Becca

Only an idiot would send a woman like that away with her husband and kid. So what, maybe I'm an idiot, but it's not like I didn't have my own reasons for doing it.

The second Jordan left, Megan dropped her nice-girl act and reminded me there were only two days left to make a decision. I think she accepted a long time ago that she was going to win this – that she had me pinned against the ropes and there was no way out. That's Megan for you: clever and cruel.

'You can't just come in and take what you want,' I said, baiting her as I loaded the dishwasher with last night's china and the porridge-crusted bowls from this morning. 'We have a whole life going on here. Something we built. Do you honestly believe you can just swoop in and claim what isn't yours? Life doesn't work like that.'

'My life does,' she said with too much sass. 'Would you rather I took Jax now?'

'I'm still giving that some thought. You promised me seven days.'

'But I made no such promise about your husband.'

It felt awful just entertaining it, but I had to get her out of the house somehow. I was pretty sure Jordan would never cheat on me, especially after hearing his explanation for what happened the other night. It also occurred to me that if he *was* cheating on me then there was nothing I could do to stop it anyway... so it might as well be useful.

'Sweet thing, if you think you can have him then you're welcome to try.'

Megan eyed me suspiciously, the challenge settling in her eyes. 'You'll regret it.'

'I regret a lot of things. That's nothing new.'

'This is your last chance. I can take him right now.'

'Better hurry. I just heard him leave.'

'Okay, you asked for this.'

That was the last thing she said before she

rushed into the guest bedroom and emerged a second later with her jacket. Megan being Megan, she shot me one last smug glare before heading out the door. The moment that door was shut, I rushed to the window and watched her interaction with Jordan. I hate the way he looks at her now – with something a lot like lust and hesitation. I feel dumb for letting this happen, but I have a task to be getting on with.

Which is why I give him the wave.

I can't imagine what's going through his mind as he walks off with Megan and our child, but at least there's not a doubt in my mind that he'll take care of our son. While I get on with my plan, I just hope he can keep it in his pants.

Because I can't lose him, too.

THE DOOR to the guest bedroom creaks open, like the mouth of a hungry monster begging me to enter. No good can come of it, but curiosity has got the better of me. We all know what that did to the cat, don't we?

I tentatively go inside, each footstep taking me closer to what I want. There's no telling whether this is going to work or not, because it's impossible

The Guest Bedroom

to know exactly what I'll find. Megan only arrived on our doorstep with one small bag, and that bag is nowhere to be seen.

Luckily, the house is empty.

Which gives me a chance to snoop.

I begin with the obvious, dropping to my knees and looking under the bed. I can smell the witch's cheap perfume on the bedding, a strawberry scent that makes me gag at the sickly teenage scent. Dark though it may be under here, I see the outline of a small box that takes my interest. Nothing should be under this bed. I should know – I designed the room myself.

It's light, practically weightless. It comes towards me as if a light wind swept it along. Without even getting up from the floor, I flip the lid and find my newspaper cuttings inside. They're scrunched up and folded in order to fit inside the box, which makes me hate her all over again. I've been looking after this stuff for years and, just like the rest of my life, she's been treating it with careless disregard.

Typical Megan.

Despite all the power she has over me, I'd much rather she didn't know I've been in here, so I replace the lid and slide the box back under. She probably won't even notice, but I need to be careful anyway. Who knows whether she'll even stick to her seven-day offer?

Offer. The word repulses me. As if my family has been a gift from her.

A gift she intends to reclaim in full.

Getting up from my knees, I rummage through the chest of drawers. There's nothing but clothes in here, a couple of snacks she's stolen from the kitchen, and two plates covered in crust that has gone hard with time. Is this the life she plans to offer Jax? A carefree mess?

No, I can't distract myself. I don't know how much time I have, so I slam the drawers shut and go to the only place that remains unchecked. The wardrobe doors open with a wooden groan, the victim of time unused. What I see before me is evidence of that, as the hangers are empty, hanging there and begging to be of purpose. There are little shelves and dividers on either side, but they're equally vacant.

Disappointed, I close the door. There's nothing here that can help my situation, which means I sent Megan to go for a walk with my family for absolutely no reason. I start to leave, then, as if from nowhere, a thought pops into my head.

The Guest Bedroom

She definitely came here with a bag.

I spin on my heel and glance around the room. Don't ask why, but the wardrobe calls to me. There's something there – something I remember asking the builder to put in at the last minute, earning an eye-roll and an irritated grunt. I rush to it now, pulling the doors open again and reaching high above my head. My palm slaps empty wood, failure growing within me inch by inch, until finally my fingers caress the rough fabric of a backpack.

Excitement explodes within me. I feel for the handle and pull it down. Unsure of what exactly it contains, I heave it over to the bed. It's heavy, definitely not empty. My mouth goes dry as I hungrily pull apart the zips and shove back the flap. There, sitting in the nook of the back pocket and promising secrets, is the one thing that might help me gain leverage. Something I knew she had but hadn't even thought to look for.

For the next few minutes, this laptop is mine.

OF COURSE THERE'S A PASSWORD.

Why wouldn't there be?

Megan is the most secretive, vindictive, manipulative woman in the entire world. Forget what you know about computer security – passwords were designed for women like her. Women who have everything to hide. And it really does make me curious.

It's a PIN password, too. Slightly easier to guess as it doesn't include the complication of upper- and lower-case characters. All it wants from me is five numbers. Too long to be an abbreviated date, too short to be a full one. I have brain lock. The only five-digit combination screaming at me is 90210, Megan's favourite show as a kid. I try that, the screen shakes as it arrogantly informs me how wrong it is, then it says I only have two attempts remaining.

It takes all my brainpower. What could be five digits? I consider Jax, myself, and Mez. I think about Jordan, but all that springs to mind is birthdays. They won't apply to this. After an irritatingly long pause, I get another idea. This time it feels more hopeful.

50501.

An inside joke created by Megan herself. She always remarked that we could split things fifty-fifty, but she would take an extra percentage for herself, making it 50/51. Or, as she always spelled

The Guest Bedroom

it, 50501. It was her goofy, childish way of saying she deserved more than others.

But it fails.

'Shit.'

One attempt remaining. What would a narcissist use as her password? Not her birthday, but something a little more *her*. Of course it wouldn't be birthdays – those are for people who care about others. Megan only cares about one thing in this whole world and that's...

'Ah.'

A laugh breaks free from my mouth as I type in the numbers like they appear on a phone or keypad: 6 for M, 3 for E, 4 for G. I keep going until her name is spelled out, hold my breath, then hit the enter button and hope for the best. The computer screen doesn't tell me I'm correct – it just lets me right into all her personal files.

You can always count on Megan to love herself.

There isn't much sitting on the desktop, but my name does stand out. I click on the file and a document opens up. A dark cloud draws over me as I skim over paragraphs of information about myself. About my *family*. There are details of my walking routines, baby groups, and times the curtains are shut so I can get in a quick nap. Jordan's working schedule is there, too, right next to the word 'HANDSOME' with a little heart next to it. I feel sick, violated, and wonder just how long she was studying us before she decided to make her move.

A while, I bet.

Tasting disgust on the tip of my tongue, I close the document and move on. The file has me curious, but there's no time for that. What I really need is something we can use – something to put her down and keep her from spilling the beans on what we did to Mez. I search high and low, but there's not a single thing except a list of coaches she could take to Collingwood. I find myself wishing I could turn back time and delete it, stopping her from ever turning up at our house. Maybe then I would still be happy. Not this scared, fragile creature I've become these past few grim, gloomy days.

Desperate, I turn to the internet. I don't have to look very far after that, because the last web page she looked at is still open. It's a news article from a place near our home town, and what it reports somehow shocks me to my core.

A baby went missing.

It's not hard to piece that together, but I read on hoping it's not true. Apparently, a woman worked herself into the lives of a happy family, posing as a nanny and earning their trust. When she was finally left alone with the baby, the parents returned home from a dinner date to find the house empty. Their nanny had vanished and, with her, their only child.

My hands are trembling all over again. My breath is weak, half held and half jittering out as I read on. Immense sympathy steals my body while I learn that the baby was later discovered on the side of the road. The six-month-old boy had been squeezed to death – suffocated by whomever had taken him. The professionals concluded that the kidnapper was mentally ill and didn't intend to kill the baby, but her desperation for being a mother had led her to hold him far tighter than a young boy could endure.

I close the laptop. My stomach turns. My hand raises to my mouth.

Megan did this. It's the only explanation. Why else would she be looking into it so deeply? Who else wants a baby more than she does and would do absolutely anything to get one? Is this how Jax will be treated if she wins. *When* she wins?

It's time I start looking at other options. It's becoming more and more apparent that my son wouldn't be safe with that psycho, and the only way to keep her away from him is to confess what happened all those years ago. Even the thought of it makes me uneasy, but the alternative is to see Jax taken away and, possibly, treated like that last boy.

I can't stand for it. Something has to change. A confession may be imminent.

There's just one last thing I want to try before that happens.

Chapter 20
Becca

While I sit in the living room and anxiously await my family's return, all I can think about is Jax. Megan absolutely *cannot* get away with this. I don't care about time pressures and bribes. Secrets don't have to be secrets if the alternative is my baby boy's death.

It makes me sick to my stomach just thinking about it.

So I think about something else.

About *her*.

She was never the same after what happened to Mez. I remember walking home with her, where we stood at my front door for far too long. She made me promise all over again that nobody would ever find out. That was when I first became aware of exactly how terrifying she was. It wasn't the shaking fear that began when she hit our friend with that rock, but the kind of cold terror that would make me sweat in my sleep for years to come. The cage was unlocked, and the monster was loose.

The following few days after Mez's murder, the whole town was asking questions. I kept watching the door in class, expecting the police to turn up. They came and went a lot, interviewing everyone Mez knew, and that included myself. It's hard to forget the way Megan put a finger to her mouth and told me to shush while I packed my bag and followed an officer into the next room. I don't know what scared me more, prison or her.

I still don't know.

A few weeks later, Megan pulled me to one side and informed me that we were safe. She said it with such excitement and pride that it made me cock my head to one side. I watched her like that for a second, then gave in to temptation and asked.

'How can you be so sure?' I said.

'Let's call it insurance.' Megan nodded, still grinning.

'What do you mean?'

'Well, you remember Mike and Josh?'

'Of course.'

'I let them do me.'

'You *what?*'

Megan gripped my arm far too tight and pulled me to the side of the school's assembly hall, where teachers and other kids cut through to reach their next classes. There, she lowered her voice. 'They both took me at the same time. Front, back, and mouth. Kind of gross, but I told them I loved having my wrists squeezed. I got Mike to hit me by telling him it turned me on. I even let them finish inside me. And now? Now they know the truth.'

I couldn't believe the little horror speaking to me. 'What truth?'

'That if they ever tell anyone they saw us that night, I'll have them done for rape.'

That was my first real taste of Megan's malicious nature. Mike and Josh were older than us and obviously didn't want to go to prison, so we never heard from them again. I didn't blame them for wanting to keep far away from that. Their whole lives hung in the balance, and all for a few minutes of fun with a deadly little psychopath.

More and more weeks rolled by, but the tension didn't alleviate. I found myself looking over my shoulder for Megan whenever I was alone. I didn't like how easy she found it to just act like nothing had ever happened. But me? I spent most of my nights crying for the loss of my friend. Mez and I were never the closest, but we got on well enough to share a giggle here or there. Some cigarettes, sometimes some alcohol, and that final exchange of looks between us as her mind raced and she wondered why I was killing her.

Christmas soon came around, and I spent the night before sitting at her empty grave. There I found her parents, who I hadn't seen since the funeral and never before that. I kept my distance by hiding behind a tree, then watched them. They bawled into each other's shoulders over the loss of their daughter. I was to blame, I remember thinking. Not just me, but at least half of it. I was a killer, and the only other person in the world who knew it was *also* a killer.

Except my first kill was accidental. Megan's wasn't.

Neither was her next one.

I HAVE to distract myself from the flood of awful, long-ago memories. My phone slides out of my pocket and into my hands with the sole intention of

The Guest Bedroom

scanning through social media to kill a few minutes while I keep an eye out the window, but then an idea comes to me from the blue.

Why don't I use this time to research a little more?

The story of the dead baby frightened the hell out of me. It's like having a massive spider on your arm – it's creeping up your skin, closer and closer to your face where it can really do some damage, but you turn your head and pray for the danger to pass. Sometimes, however, you need to get a good look at the spider. Know your enemies, I've heard people say, which is why I'm quickly putting the murder through a search engine.

There's plenty of information; professional articles, freelancers, videos, and even some sick jokes made for the video apps. I swallow in disgust and start bookmarking the ones that are better summarised. Every second I spend thinking about this story makes me feel more nauseous, until I have to send my phone to the lock screen and put it down.

Right on cue, there's movement outside the window. Jordan is pushing the pram, and I sigh a breath of relief to see Jax world-facing, his head resting on his own shoulder as he dozes peacefully.

For a fleeting moment, I see something else in him – a dead baby and the lunatic beside him who'd done the ultimate evil. Then he stirs, and I turn my attention to Megan. She's still beaming as if she doesn't have a care in the world, and her rose-painted nails are still all over my husband. The only consolation is that he does look truly uncomfortable.

As if that will help me sleep at night.

Jordan unlocks the door, and Megan storms through first. She goes straight for the guest bedroom and slides off her jacket, but not without giving me an evil sneer first. I've never hated a human being as much as I do right now. *Is* she even human? Could a real person actually do all these awful things to not just one family but two? I certainly couldn't. Not even if it meant saving myself. Or Jordan or Jax, for that matter. It just isn't in me.

As soon as she goes into the room, I become a little nervous. My foot starts tapping away on the window seat, and I gnaw my fingernails and watch my husband struggle with the buggy. Jax starts to stir, and I should be rushing forward to help. It's so strange – all I can do is observe and get an eyeful of them as they are. Is this how I'll remember them?

The Guest Bedroom

Not for the glorified moments like our son's birth or the first time his father held him, but for something as simple as wrestling with a buggy through a doorway?

I look at the guest bedroom again, wondering if Megan has figured it out. If she knows I've gone through her things. Regardless of whether she has or hasn't, there's a very finite window in which I can act on what I found. Sure, it can wait until tonight, but we're getting far too close to the deadline. Time is running out ever so fast, and I don't want to waste a second.

It's time to tell him.

As soon as the front door is shut, I push myself up from the window seat and approach Jordan. Jax is opening his eyes, staring around the place to figure out what time and space he's awoken in. I scoop him into my arms and sniff his hair, getting a waft of cinnamon while I nod towards the kitchen. Jordan raises an eyebrow but follows anyway.

'It's hard to believe you encouraged that walk,' he says. 'Megan is about as fun as a bag of testicles. Did you know she told me I'm cute seven times? Seven!'

It really doesn't surprise me, but her compliments towards my husband are the least of my worries. I'm busy peering around the corner as Jax wriggles in my arms, making sure the door to the guest bedroom is properly shut. Satisfied (for now), I hand my phone to Jordan and watch as he concentrates on the article. It takes somewhere between five and ten minutes to read through it all, absorbing the intense content just like I did earlier – feeling the disgusted and bizarre emotions exactly the same way I had to. By the time he's finished, he looks exhausted. He hands the phone back with an exasperated breath.

'I think I've heard about this before,' he says. 'But not in such great detail.'

The phone is placed in my hand, and I pocket it real fast. 'At work?'

'No, just in the news or maybe on the grapevine.'

'And your opinion as a police officer?'

'Is... what?' Jordan shrugs. 'I didn't exactly review the case. Why?'

'Because I think the woman who did it is Megan.'

His mouth gapes open like I just used the C-word. Trust me, I've been tempted, but all that's

The Guest Bedroom

really happened is I hit him with the truth. No more messing around, just straight out with what I think happened and... well, and *is* happening.

'Isn't that a little extreme?' he asks.

'Not if you know Megan.'

'Then why did you let her into our home?'

'I only just found this.'

Jordan opens his mouth in an ah-ha manner and raises his chin. 'Now I get it. That's why you wanted her to come out for a walk with me, isn't it? So you could go rifling through her stuff? I've got to say, I'm a little disappointed.'

'You can be as disappointed as you like, as long as you believe me.'

'What exactly makes you think it's her?'

'It was plastered all over her computer.'

'So? You'll find a ton of porn on *my* computer. Doesn't make me a porn star.'

'I'm serious.' I take another look at the bedroom door. Still shut, thankfully. 'Think about it. She finally left our home town after all these years. She desperately wants to become a mum. She has a history of violence and—'

'Excuse me?' Jordan holds up a hand, like he's on patrol and stopping a car. The humour has lost his face, now replaced by deep concern. No, not just concern – regret. 'You mean to tell me there's a woman in our house who has a history of violence, you suspect has killed a baby, and you haven't done a single thing to get her out?'

I shake my head and swallow. My mouth is horribly dry. 'I know how it sounds.'

'How it sounds it that you need to get yourself together. Megan is a little on the loopy side, and I don't altogether trust her, but you're accusing her of being a kidnapper and a baby murderer. You understand the seriousness of those statements, don't you? Especially seeing as you're talking to a police officer.'

'You don't have to believe me—'

'Damn right.'

'But can you at least do me a favour and look into it?'

'Look into... Becca, what power do you think I have exactly?'

'I don't know. You must have some resources. Software or records or something.'

There's a long, painful pause while Jordan rubs his chin and stares at the kitchen floor. Jax starts babbling, and heat rises to my cheeks when the guest bedroom door opens. Megan lingers behind it, watching but just out of earshot. Desperate, I

The Guest Bedroom

look at my husband and pray he comes out with the smart decision – the right thing to do.

'I'll make a deal with you,' he says.

'Anything.'

'I'll take a look – a small one – and if you're right then I'll handle it.'

'Why does it feel like there's more to this deal?'

'Because there is.' He moves in close and whispers in my ear. 'If you're wrong, I want you to apologise to Megan, seek professional help, and explain to me whatever it is you've been hiding these past few days.'

It's easy to agree. The extra pair of eyes on Megan is going to help immensely, and I know that in two days – no matter the outcome – none of the things he said will matter to me. Because if I'm right about Megan then I'll have something to bargain with.

If I'm wrong, I'll be in prison anyway.

Chapter 21
Jordan

I HAVE my doubts about Megan, which is to say Becca's theory is starting to fester. As a police officer you learn an awful lot about procedure, but you're very much limited to the chronology of that process. In the real world – the place outside of that where you act as a human being with emotions and just good sense – you can tell a thousand things about a person just by using the one thing the law won't allow you to pursue.

A hunch.

Megan is a shady character. There are no two ways about it. Maybe I've been seeing through rose-tinted glasses these past few days because, whether or not I'd like to admit it, our guest has stirred something in my loins. It's the possibility of some excitement outside of my marriage (no matter how forcefully I sought to ignore these feelings) that made me take it easy on Megan. Really, she doesn't deserve it, because I realise now.

I don't know the first thing about her.

I mean, she's been flirting with me. Exciting as that is, she's been doing it with complete disregard to her so-called friend. I never had the best role models, but it's pretty obvious that if you're staying under a friend's roof then you shouldn't try sleeping with her husband.

That tells me all I need to know about her.

Becca has gone upstairs now, changing Jax's nappy and giving me a few minutes of peace before work. I'm in my uniform, keys in my pocket and ready to go, but something feels unfinished. I shoot a quick look at the guest bedroom door, which is ajar with some Alanis Morissette singing peacefully from inside. It's now I realise there's something I want to test.

'Megan?' I say, rapping gently on the door while pushing it open.

'Have you come to arrest me, officer?'

Megan is lying on the bed with her phone held above her. Her head has rotated to look me up and down, a flirtatious smile carved on to her lips. The jeans she's wearing are too tight, and certain parts of her are... let's say 'discernible' through the denim.

'Not exactly. My laptop is playing up. Can I use yours for a few minutes?'

Then comes the exact reaction I was hoping to see. She sits bolt upright and her face flushes red. Her hands start anxiously working, tossing her phone just an inch or two into the air and catching it, over and over. Trying to look relaxed. Failing miserably.

'Wish I could help, but I don't have a laptop,' she says.

'You don't? I thought I remembered seeing you with one.'

'No. Must have been dreaming.'

'Must have.'

'Do you often dream about me?'

I smile politely and reach for the door handle. 'See you soon.'

With that behind me, I reach for my keys and head out to the car. It's not proof of her wrongdoing, but I trust my wife enough to believe her when she says she used Megan's laptop. I don't know exactly why she would deny having one, but it adds to the pile of reasons to be suspicious. Feeling

The Guest Bedroom

how I feel about her now, it feels wrong leaving them in a house together.

I hesitate by the door, think about asking Becca if she'll be okay, then realise that might be blowing things out of proportion. Megan may be dodgy, but I think some of my wife's paranoia might be down to a bit of post-partum. I'll have to trust that everything will be okay.

Hopefully, I won't regret this.

As PER USUAL, work is only adding to my stress.

I've got problems with two quarrelling neighbours in town. A drunkard who keeps appearing outside the local school with an affinity for public masturbation. My boss is breathing down my neck because I'm yet to catch up on files for a string of recent break-ins.

Yet all I can think about is Megan.

It's not in the same way I used to think about her. The excitement for her is gone, replaced by nothing but suspicion. Even if what Becca said was completely wrong, I don't like the way those two are bouncing off each other. There's something hidden between the two of them. Something toxic, and no good can ever come of something like that.

Besides, I promised I would look into this.

I make a call to a friend who lives in that neck of the woods. We haven't had a proper conversation in years, but we occasionally call in a favour and there are no questions asked. It's more like a professional relationship than a friendship really, and that's fine because after a few minutes of convincing him, he allows me access to all the information he has on that kidnapping case, putting it on my computer as if by remote.

'I'd be careful with this one,' he says. 'It might turn your gut a little.'

'Thanks for the heads-up.'

I felt brave when I took it, but my friend was right. There are crime scene photos of the baby who was found on the side of the road. Discarded like a chocolate bar wrapper. The bumps and bruises suggest he was hurled out of a moving car, and suddenly I've lost my appetite. I pass by the images having seen all I need to see, then move on to the police files.

Very little is known about the woman who took the child. There isn't so much as a single photo of her. The names don't match, but the descriptions do. Everything down to Megan's eye colour. I rest my elbow on the desk and stare beyond the screen, deep in thought as I nibble at my knuckles. A chill runs through me like a winter river, making me shudder.

Is a baby killer in our home?

Becca would never let that happen... would she?

I feel conflicted. There's not a whole lot of evidence to suggest that Megan and this monster are the same person, but my care for Jax encourages me to ignore my evergrowing to-do list and dig a little deeper. I don't give a damn how long it takes or how much trouble I get in for ignore my duties as an officer.

Because I'm seriously starting to worry Becca was right.

Chapter 22
Becca

It no longer feels like my home.

While Jordan is out putting in a day's work while (with any luck) investigating the dead baby case, I'm stuck at home with a nutcase who wants to take my son. I'm doing my best to stay out of her way, but she keeps following me around the house.

It started in the laundry room, where she stands behind me and offers to take care of Jax. Not a single force in this world could make me agree to that, so instead I let him crawl around and examine the clothing pegs and bottom of the inactive radiator. It's bad parenting – I know that – but it's better than the other option.

I make a rush job of throwing the washing in the machine while keeping a keen eye on him, then

The Guest Bedroom

I leave the wash basket behind and pick up my son, heading for the kitchen to prepare his lunch in advance. Of course, Megan follows me like a fly in pursuit of hot food, and I can't seem to be rid of that dreadful buzzing.

'Why don't you let me prepare his food?' Megan asks from the doorway.

'Because I'm very capable,' I tell her, the tap running as I reach for a chopping board.

'I'm just saying, I might as well get the practice in as he'll be mine soon.'

I stab her with a scornful look, then get slicing up toast and broccoli so Jax can digest them. Just the thought of this woman having my son is enough to send me into a blind rage, but I must contain myself – I must exercise a little control.

The little witch lingers in the room the whole time I'm feeding Jax. It's weird how I suddenly feel too uncomfortable to even talk to my son in the usual gibberish babble, but I'm so conscious of Megan being in the room. I know exactly what she's doing – she's applying pressure, like an animal playing with its food. I certainly feel like the prey.

After that, it's time to start an hour or so of playtime. Something just enough to keep his brain active and tire him out. Then he'll be ready for his midday nap. I'm exhausted, too, but I don't much feel like sleeping. I'd probably have to do it with one eye open.

It's getting too intense. I need some air. Some breathing space. I start thinking about taking Jax into the car and just driving non-stop. Can I run away from home that way, so far that the police wouldn't find me even if Megan did decide to reveal my big secret? Or has she been bluffing this whole time? Does she really not care about me bringing her down with me, or has she somehow got that covered and found a way to put all the blame on me?

No, I have to go. I'll miss Jordan dearly, but maybe I'll be back in a few days. Megan might give up when she realises I'm willing to leave, so why not at least give it a try and see how it goes? I glance out the window and see the car – the Punto we only really use for emergencies. It would be so easy to get up and go.

'Why do you keep looking out the window?' Megan asks.

'No reason,' I tell her.

'You keep looking at the car.'

The Guest Bedroom

'Thinking of going for a drive, is all. A short one.'

'Hmm...'

It's enough to get her off my back, but not enough to make me comfortable. I haul Jax up into my arms, give him a kiss, then get him ready for his nap. Perhaps afterwards I'll take the keys and just go. No packing, no food, just me and the empty road.

Whatever it takes to get away from Megan.

Jax's nap is the longest two hours of my life.

I've started fantasising about my new life. Jordan is in it – he's caught us somewhere up the road and agreed to come with us. In one version of this alternative future, he's even discovered my big secret... and he's okay with it. 'Accidents happen,' he would say, then explain that he knows my true character and is dead certain I would never intentionally harm another human being. What would that mean for me in a legal sense? Manslaughter? Obstruction of justice? I don't know enough about the law to comment, but it's my fantasy.

I make the rules.

I've almost made it sound appealing. Any future without Megan in it *is* appealing. All I have to do is get past her. To somehow get in the car without her following me like a shadow. I spend my time formulating a plan that really can't get more elaborate than simply climbing into the car and hoping for the best. All the while, I'm sitting in the dark room and watching the black outline of my son. I love him so dearly – the way his tiny chest expands as he takes wheezy little breaths. My heart is pounding when it hits me what I'm about to do to him.

I'm about to uproot his entire life.

The only good thing is that he'll never remember it. He's so young that he doesn't really have any idea what's going on. He'll never remember this house, and I'm not sure if that makes me relieved or depressed. It's not fair that we're forced into doing this – that we had a perfect life together as a happy little family, and now there's no option but to leave without so much as a single bag on our backs. Except for the baby bag, I guess.

That's when I get the idea of throwing some spare clothes into that. Without waking Jax, I take the bag and head to my bedroom, then start stuffing some necessary items inside. The monitor is still

The Guest Bedroom

buzzing on the bedside table, white noise hissing through the speaker as my baby starts to stir. A bead of sweat forms on my brow. I wipe it away with my sleeve and zip up the bag. We're ready to go. I take a breath, barely able to believe we're doing this.

Jax starts screaming now. A fragile, gentle scream for his mummy. I go to him before Megan can beat me to it, holding him to my chest and taking one last look around the room. This isn't the end, I tell myself, mostly just to inspire a little courage. I'll be back, reunited with Jordan after Megan leaves for good. Hopefully, with her tail between her legs.

Everything ready to go, we head downstairs. Megan is in the living room, so I take the long way around through the kitchen and laundry room, where the washing machine is starting to shout as the spin intensifies. My lungs feel tight as I realise I'm holding my breath, so I let it go and peer around the corner. Megan hasn't moved – she's still sitting there calmly, playing with her phone while some cheesy pop sings from the speaker. Somehow, she's gone from harassing me constantly to not even caring that I exist.

It's making me paranoid.

At last, we make it to the front door. I'm half-expecting her to come bounding after us, merrily inviting herself on our road trip. I get lucky, and no such thing happens. It's just me and Jax, a few short feet between us and freedom. I can barely believe my luck when I unlock the car and strap him into the seat. He doesn't even put up a fight – it's as simple as buckling up, kissing him gently on the forehead, then reaching for the door handle.

That's when I see it.

The front tyre is flat.

Not just flat, but *shredded*. There's a gaping hole in the rubber, the edges course and rough. All hope floods out of me, a hollow opening in my stomach. I brush my hair back and groan, then catch sight of the rear tyre. Also slashed.

My disappointment turns to anger. Anger leads to pure hate. I get the idea to walk around the car, inspecting the other tyres. Number three, also slashed. Number four, torn to shreds. It's not an accident, and nor has it been intended to look that way. Megan must have got the sense that I was trying to flee, and she not only prevented my escape but wanted me to know about it. Now, here I am, standing in the sun with my baby in the car and nothing but fear in my heart.

Any hope I did have is long gone.

Just like everything else, Megan has taken that from me.

I DON'T KNOW what to do. My entire day (and all the coming days in my near future) were mapped out. I was going to take a lump sum from the bank and then keep driving, paying for hotels along the way in cash and staying off the radar while I waited for what would happen with the police. If God decided to bless me with a rare break, the coast would be clear, Megan would realise she couldn't get anything from me, and she'd move on to a new town. Then I could return to my husband and carry on with the carefree life I was enjoying until recently.

Now, all of that is out the window.

I stare at the tyres with ire raging in my heart. The house's front door opens, and Megan pokes her head around the corner. She looks like a deadly snake – venomous and sly – that eerie smile working its demonic magic all over again. I shiver when I see her.

'Something wrong?' she asks, and she knows damn well something is wrong.

'What did you do to my tyres?' I say, ignoring her question.

'Me? I haven't done anything. I've been in the living room all morning.'

'We both know that's not true.'

Megan shrugs, props an umbrella in the door to keep it from closing, then steps into the sun. Golden rays kiss her black hair, looking like fire on charred wood. She comes closer, her hands digging into her shallow jeans pockets as she looks at the mess she created.

'That looks terrible,' she says as if she doesn't know how it happened.

'You didn't have to do this.' I'm trying not to cry. 'I just wanted a break.'

'Ah, that's not true.'

'What?'

'You were thinking of running away with my baby, weren't you?'

Her baby? I feel so protective that I shove past her and lean against the door where Jax is starting to cry. I keep my back to it and train my sight on her. Disgust and panic spark within me. '*My* baby, you creep. And so what if I wanted to go somewhere?'

Megan shakes her head and tuts. 'I told you

before, this is going to happen whether you like it or not. I mean, you can try refusing me if you want, but you'll end up behind bars.'

'So will you!'

'It really doesn't bother me. If I don't have Jax then it doesn't matter what happens.'

'You're really willing to give up your whole life for the sake of someone else's kid?'

'Obviously. Why does it even bother you so much?'

'Because he's my son, you sadistic cretin.'

'Which means nothing. It's not like you can't pop out another sprog.'

I don't know why it's taken me so long to see this, but Megan really can't tell the difference between possession and love. The way she's suggesting I just give up one kid and produce another is insane. It's like she thinks I can just clone Jax and carry on with life like normal. Business as usual in the baby-making industry, right?

Megan huffs out a breath and then points to her wrist, the non-existent watch taking a tap from her finger. 'You've got one more day,' she says. 'Even less than that if you keep trying to worm your way out of this. Honestly, you're trying my patience.'

I say nothing because there's nothing *to* say. This utterly mad woman will do anything to take Jax, and she even has the audacity to make a joke of it as she trudges back to the house. She pauses in the doorway just long enough to mouth some words to me, then disappears inside while I replay them in my mind – her sick, raspy voice repeating on a horrifying loop.

'Tick-tock,' it says. 'Tick-tock, tick-tock.'

Chapter 23
Becca

I should have seen this coming from a mile off. Megan was never going to let me leave. She must have known from day one that I would try something like that. It's quite possible that she'd even prepared the knife to slice through the tyres with.

I was never allowed to escape.

As I begrudgingly begin to retrieve Jax from the car, I can't help thinking about those years in between Mez's murder and now. Every one of Megan's moves suggested she was not to be trusted, and I was the idiot who just stood there and let it all happen. All of those incidents that went unreported. All of those murders I'm certain were her doing.

It started with a man in his late twenties.

Megan confided in me that she was seeing this man (she was only eighteen at the time and, although technically legal, it had some questionable suspension of morals) and that he loved her dearly.

'It's nuts,' she told me with childish glee. 'He'll buy me anything and all I have to do is spread my legs. Same as most men. Really makes you think, doesn't it?'

Well, I disagreed. Not to her face – I was far too afraid of her for that – but I didn't like the way men were being generalised and disrespected. It was bad enough her world was starting to turn that way, but Megan in particular was putting them down while siphoning money from their accounts and failing to see how she was the bad guy.

That man eventually killed himself. Jumped off a train bridge if you can believe the irony. It was written in his suicide note that he loved Megan so much that it hurt and, despite being able to give her all the money in the world, he couldn't give her a baby. That was why she'd left him, and the poor soul didn't know what to do with that heartache.

If only he knew it was *her* body preventing pregnancy.

Megan fell through the legal loophole and wasn't able to take a single penny as inheritance.

The Guest Bedroom

That was clearly the biggest thing on her mind, because she never mentioned him again, didn't even turn up to his funeral, and had a new boyfriend within the week. I kept a close eye on this one, Megan feeding me the details on an almost nightly basis as if we were best friends again. In reality, I wanted nothing more than to run far away from her and never look back. Perhaps that would come eventually, but not now.

This unfortunate man's name was Arthur, and he was the same age as us. If his tattered, skater-boy clothing was anything to go by, he didn't have any money either. What he *did* have was his own flat, which Megan spent every night in. To use her own words, she was 'riding his disco stick' and hoping for the fertility gods to bless her. This went on for months, which led to a year, and then Arthur mysteriously disappeared.

The police were searching for ages. They interviewed Megan, of course, who played the part of heartbroken girlfriend all too well. When his body turned up face down in a pond with stab wounds all over his chest, it became a national news piece. Megan somehow managed to avoid not only the blame but also heat from the press. That always struck me as a miracle considering she was the one who'd stabbed him. I know that for a fact.

Because she told me.

Not that I could do anything about it. Megan still knew my secret, and that was being used against me. I started questioning my own morals then, withholding the truth because I didn't want to end up in jail. I disgusted myself, but not enough to actually report what she'd said to me. Besides, there would be no proof. It wasn't like she'd forewarned me that she was going to confess a murder. Much less with a weird amount of pride.

At least I figured out how she managed to stay out of trouble. Her next physical conquest was a police officer. She was turning twenty then, and he was a married man. Megan freely told me that she was getting bent over the desk by him and then she was threatening to tell his wife if they didn't at least try for a baby. This one gave me the chills because I knew she was capable of murder. Not just murder, but lying and blackmail and everything in between. It was like she was a totally different person to the friend I went to school with. No longer a young woman at all, but a monster. Who isn't afraid of monsters?

The last time I saw that cop, Megan was

hanging from his arm in the street. She introduced the two of us, but he had no interest in me whatsoever. He looked absolutely appalled, like he didn't want to be there and was scared people might see the two of them together. I remember the way he looked over his shoulders as Megan informed me that they were having a baby together and she was going to raise it on her own. That was the biggest shock of my life. At least at the time.

Sadly, she miscarried just three months later. The doctors said her womb was inhospitable and it was an act of God that she even managed to become pregnant in the first place. Well, for someone like Megan, that news wasn't just devastating but indescribably infuriating. She didn't react well – she told the cop's wife everything that had happened, then played dumb when the cop eventually disappeared.

How she was getting away with all of this I'll never know, but my actions probably held some influence. Megan grabbed me by the wrist one night and told me I had to be her alibi for the night the cop went missing. I wasn't about to tell her no – not after knowing what I knew – so I went along with it and she went under the radar yet again.

Megan and I began to distance then. There

was no telling what was cooking in her head, so I stayed as far away as possible. It quickly became apparent that if I ever wanted to be rid of her fully, I'd need to pack up and move towns. Maybe get married and change my surname. It would be almost impossible to find me then, so I'd do my best to make it a reality.

Because I never wanted to see that woman again.

This is it. I've had enough.

My life has been too up in the air lately. I haven't had a single minute where I've been able to settle because I simply don't feel safe. What I need is for someone to believe me when I tell them how much trouble Megan is. It doesn't mean my past sins need to come to light just yet, but it's barely something I care about any more. After reliving the nightmare from all those years ago, all I can think about is Jax's safety. My own situation is no longer relevant.

That's the choice I made when I became a mother.

Knowing just what to do, I head inside the house. Megan has returned to the sofa as if nothing has happened these past few minutes, which only makes her seem creepier. Neither of us say anything as I pass, clutching Jax in my arms and finding a place for him in the kitchen high chair. Not that he needs to eat just yet.

But I need to make a call.

Taking a quick check to ensure Megan hasn't moved, I pick up my phone and scroll through looking for Jordan's name. My breathing is short and desperate as I go past his name multiple times, then quickly hit the dial button. It rings and rings, but he doesn't pick up. That's unusual for him, unless he's completely snowed under with work.

Or with research on Megan.

Speaking of which, I peer around the door frame once more and find her still sitting there, her face buried in her phone as she scrolls through social media. The frantic beating inside my chest only intensifies as the automated woman's voice on the phone tells me to leave my message. She seems to waffle on for a lifetime before it's my turn to speak.

I cross the kitchen, half-smile at Jax, then whisper into the phone.

'Jordan, it's me. Things are getting really bad, and I need you to come home. I wanted to leave and... well, I was getting ready to use the car when the tyres were torn open. All of them. It's Megan. She was always the problem and...' I close my eyes and take a deep breath. 'I've decided I'll tell you everything. Just please come home. We're not safe here right n—'

'You sneaky little bitch!'

Megan's voice erupts from behind me. I gasp and end the call without thinking, like a girl hiding the cookie jar with her hand still inside it. Across the kitchen, that nightmarish woman is snarling, her upper lip straining to reveal her teeth as she glares at me in disgust. My weak, trembling fingers lose their grip on the phone. Then, as if to punish me for my actions, she storms towards me. I quickly look down and see it right away.

Her fists are clenched.

Jax must pick up on the mood in the room, because he starts to cry. It breaks my heart to hear him so upset, and I want to go to him. I take two short steps, but then Megan cuts me off by holding an arm out straight between me and my son.

'I need to help him,' I state as a matter of fact.

'That won't be happening.'

The Guest Bedroom

'Please, Megan. You can't—'

'Don't you *dare* tell me what I can or cannot do!'

Megan's finger jolts out and jerks me between the ribs. A pained breath bursts from my mouth as I cover my chest and step back, shock taking over. Megan closes the distance within a second, her face scrunched up like a devilish menace who's been scorned. I just wish she could see – I'm not the one who's being awful here.

She is.

'I tried to help you,' she spits through clenched teeth, stepping closer towards me as I stumble back. 'I tried to be nice to you by giving you seven days to make the right decision, and this is how you repay me? By telling your cop husband that you'll explain all this to him?'

Jax's cry turns into a scream. I want to scream, too, but keeping a brave face is important. Which makes it so much worse that I'm failing this miserably – I want to cry, or at least fight back, but I'm frozen stiff by the icy touch of fear seizing my entire body.

'Megan, please just let me comfort my child.'

'No.' She shakes her head adamantly. 'He's not your child.'

'You're scaring him. Please...'

That's all I manage to say, because she lashes out at me then. She lunges forward and grabs my top, pulling it with such force that I tumble past her. Pain explodes up my back as she punches it, once, twice, then hurls me at the kitchen counter. I lose my balance. Jax's screams grow to deafening wails as he helplessly watches his mother attacked. It all happens too fast to process any sort of emotion, and Megan throws me to the floor.

'Stay down!' she screams like a banshee, right in my face.

Her knuckles strike my head one after the other. Unable to gain any leverage, I cover my head. My forearms take the beating as I try bringing my knees to my chest, only to kick her away. But Megan is stronger than I am, and she has much more experience with violence. That is to say I have none, whereas she lives and breathes it.

The kitchen is filled with screams and shouting. Jax is in trouble. *I'm* in trouble, and the only break from this danger comes in the few short seconds where Megan stands and reaches for something on the counter. I freeze just long enough to realise she's grabbed the glass fruit bowl, but I can't react fast enough. It comes down in a lightning-blow that strikes my skull.

People often tell of stories like this, where time slows down but they also have no control. That's what's happening to me, except there's one difference. I'm not going to awake from this, because the white-hot sudden pain erupts all over my skull as the glass shatters and the world turns black. I'm only alive long enough to hear Jax scream one last time.

And to know I'll never hold him again.

Chapter 24
Becca

It's amazing what goes through your head when you think you're dying. The very fact that thoughts are, in fact, being processed serves as clarification that you're still alive. Maybe not awake or conscious, but alive. That's something, right?

Lying there on the kitchen floor, with the cold tiles pressing roughly against my back and head, a fire rages through my scalp. It burns like the seventh circle of hell, and it feels like I'm still flinching at the fruit bowl being swung at me. Other than myself, there's only one person to blame for all of this.

Megan.

My mind drifts back to when I left that town. My mother was talking about leaving anyway,

The Guest Bedroom

since we hadn't seen my dad in a number of years and it didn't look like he was coming back. She told me she was going to start a new life and wanted me to move close to her, but that she didn't want me living in the same actual house. You've got to understand I was twenty-one, homeless, being asked to move, and had no job prospects whatsoever. Worse than that, I was scared – scared to leave. Scared to stay.

Terrified of how Megan would react.

That was the reason I never told her about my intentions. I didn't actually tell *anyone* where I was going. People in town would surely talk about where my mother was going (people tended to gossip about this kind of stuff), and that could get back to my enemy, so I thought why not go a few extra miles and move on to a little town called Collingwood? It was about a two-hour drive from my mother, which was close enough to keep her happy and far enough that it would be hard to find me.

I started working in the local shop of this small town, stacking shelves and serving customers on the till. My manager was – for lack of a better term – a complete and utter arsehole who spoke to me like a sexual object. This went on for months before a handsome stranger stepped in to make him adjust his behaviour. My employer fired me, of course, but I managed to leave safely and with the smallest shred of dignity.

That man introduced himself as Jordan and offered to buy me lunch. I jumped at the chance and sat to eat with him. He was my age, tall, handsome, and in very good shape. He told me he was joining the local police and couldn't wait to make a difference. I fell in love with his personality right away, and we soon became an item.

I spent some time hopping from job to job until my father was confirmed to have died of cancer. It turned out he had some hefty inheritance to leave behind, which my mother and I split equally. As horrible as it sounds, it was good timing – because Jordan and I wanted a baby but first we had to try living together to see how it worked. And it did work.

Really well.

Over time, I began to forget about Megan. As even more years whipped by, I even stopped thinking about Mez altogether. That life was behind me, a thing of the past that I had no intention of revisiting. Here, in Collingwood, was the brand-new Becca. A good woman, a doting wife, and a soon-to-be mother who just wanted to be at peace.

You already know the rest of the story.

At least, everything up until now.

WHEN I WAKE UP PROPERLY, the whole room is spinning. A weird, numbing sensation tickles my tongue as my limp hand reaches out for something to grab on to. It's like waking up with a hangover, except the memories of how you ended up here come flooding back in a torrent.

'Jax,' I mumble in my panicked, half-aware state.

Turning my head to one side, I can see the high chair. My son's tiny legs dangle from within the seat, his socked little toes a sight to behold. I rush to my feet, desperately holding on to the kitchen drawer handles to heave myself up. There's no sign of Megan whatsoever, which can only be a good sign. At least she left without my baby.

My legs are like jelly. My knees threaten to give out as I transfer weight to them. It's not perfect, but I'm up. Before I know it, I'm stumbling towards Jax and wondering how long ago he stopped crying. It pains me to think that he gave up on the idea of me helping him and has now cried his way into silence. No baby should have to go through that. Certainly not mine.

The room is still spiralling as I reach the high chair. Dizzy, I reach for my son and grasp only air. My hands missed their mark, so I try again but only then realise the chair is empty. I must have hallucinated when I saw his feet, and now the high chair is not the only vacant spot in the room. A gaping hole has torn inside my heart, my chest feeling tight as I roam my gaze around the kitchen, hoping this has all just been one horrible dream.

'Jax?' I whimper, meek and lethargic. 'Megan?'

I stumble into the living room, leaning against all the hallway furniture as I search for any sign of life. The house is so quiet it makes me sick. Or perhaps that's the dizziness talking. Regardless, I call out Megan's name and pray she'll come waltzing out of a room with Jax in her arms. Maybe in this fantasy she could even be apologetic, understand things have gone too far, then hand over my son and leave, never to return again.

None of that happens. Instead, I find myself slowly moving between the rooms, shouting my son's name. He's too young to respond, but with some luck he might hear his mother's voice and

The Guest Bedroom

start crying for attention. I'll take anything at this point – any way to let me know where he is and how I can hold him safely in my arms again. Whatever it takes.

But there's nothing.

I've searched the whole house high and low. I check again, my energy slowly returning to me as pain splinters across my head. Except the pain no longer bothers me. It's the aching chasm in my life that's taken my attention. As I enter the nursery on a second and final tour of the house, it occurs to me that I've been so busy looking for people that I didn't even think to look at their possessions. Jax has a bag and buggy. Megan has a room full of things.

Heat rising to my cheeks, I hurry back downstairs. My feet thunder along the floorboards as I pound my way to the front door. The buggy is gone, its usual resting place empty. The bag is missing, too, and all my deepest fears are coming to life. Tears blurring my vision, I dash towards the guest bedroom and weep as soon as the door swings open.

Because Megan's things are gone.

Megan is gone.

And she's taken my baby with her.

. . .

I'm a bag of nerves, biting the nails off my quivering fingers as I stare blurry-eyed at the carpet. I want to throw up, but my body won't let me. I want to keep moving just to work off some of my nervous energy, but I also want to stay still. All hope and happiness has left me along with my son. I'm not even fully recovered from the blow I took, and my world has just shattered.

I need help.

Jax needs help.

Suddenly recalling the attack in the kitchen, I'm struck by the memory of my phone hitting the floor. My feet are moving before I can even process the thought fully, and I'm on my hands and knees in the kitchen looking for the phone. There's a mess of glass that pierces my knees as I scan around the tiles, but I don't care. My entire world is falling apart, and I don't even have the means to call the police – to call Jordan.

I'm breaking down again, the tears coming back with a vengeance. I choke on them, my bloody hand clapping over my mouth as the realisation pummels into me again and again: my son is gone, my son is gone, *my son is gone!*

The Guest Bedroom

But there's no time for self-pity. Jax needs me, and I'll never be able to live with myself if I let anything bad happen to him. This spurs me on to my feet, where I snatch my house keys from the bowl by the front door and sprint through town towards the police station. Along the way, people see the state of me and ask if I'm okay. There's no time to stop and explain, so I just yell at them to call the police because my son is missing.

My son is *missing*.

I reach the station in minutes. Who knows how far Megan has gone in that time? If you factor in the time I was unconscious – God only knows how long that was – she could be far out of Collingwood by now. How the hell am I going to explain this to Jordan? Even if he has listened to my voicemail, to which there's no guarantee, I've got a lot of backstory to give before we can start figuring out where Megan has taken our beautiful baby boy.

The doors bust open as I run inside. There's a small gathering of people standing in reception, and a couple of people are seated. I ignore them all, not giving a crap who hears my story as I hit the desk to stop myself. The lady across the desk looks at me over her glasses.

'I need to report a kidnapping,' I bark at her.

'Young lady, there's a procedure that—'

'Tell Officer Baxter his son is missing.'

The mere mention of my husband's name makes her take this more seriously. Her entire demeanour changes, the grey ringlets of craggy hair being blown aside with an annoyed puff from the fifty-something, stick-up-her-own-arse desk sergeant.

'How do you know Officer Baxter?'

'I'm his wife.'

'Is he expecting you?'

'What? No. Please, just go get him.'

'Watch your tone, will you? Why don't you calmly explain to me—'

'I don't have the time to bloody explain!' I snap, the anxiety and urgency blasting out of me in a furious outburst. 'Someone smashed a goddamn fruit bowl over my head and took my son. Now will you stop with the power games and go get my husband?'

The woman barely has time to react before a door beside me opens. Jordan's superior comes out, a file in his hand and a look of utter confusion on his face. When he sees it's me causing the commotion, he seems to settle. We've only met each other a handful of times – mostly at the police station

The Guest Bedroom

Christmas parties – but we have no trouble recognising each other.

'Mrs. Baxter,' he says in the deep, husky voice that promises reassurance.

'Please can I speak to Jordan?'

'I'm afraid that's not possible.'

The woman beside me grunts with satisfaction, but I pay her no mind. She's of little importance to me. In fact, everything is of absolutely no importance whatsoever until Jax is returned safely to my arms. Only then can I deal with the consequences.

Jordan's superior, whose name I've misplaced in a frantic rush to find my husband, places a hand gently on my elbow and encourages me to the side of the room. There, he lowers his voice and explains to me that Jordan left some time ago. Apparently, he grabbed his keys and ran for the door without so much as a word to anyone.

'Why?' I ask. 'Why would he do that?'

'All I know is that he looked sick with worry. Any idea what it's about?'

I nod but don't explain. It's possible he found what he was looking for when looking into the case of the murdered baby. But if that's true, wouldn't he rush home and check on us? Wouldn't he pick up his phone to call me, then find the voicemail I left for him?

'Mrs. Baxter?' the man says, then points to exactly where the fire seems to be forming on my bleeding forehead. 'Can I get you a glass of water and tend to that wound?'

I wave it off and shake my head, then tell him no.

There are more pressing matters at hand.

I need to find my son.

Chapter 25
Jordan

I was torn between gathering the evidence to make an arrest and heading back home to my wife and kid. Their safety is everything to me, but how much of a danger can Megan really be? She'd been in our home this whole time and hasn't hurt anyone yet. I decided to grant myself just one hour to find what I could and then head home to check on Becca.

As time went on, I began to stress. The witness statements from the dead baby's mother were extremely long and erratic – as they had every right to be – making them hard to follow. I found myself having to reread certain passages as my heart broke at the unimaginable pain those parents had gone through. It made me think of Jax and what I might do if anything ever happened to him. Like most people, I imagine I'd kill to protect him, but for some that is nothing more than a hypothetical situation.

But the way they spoke about their nanny...

It did sound like Megan, but in description only. If you changed the hair colour – something easily fixed with a bottle of dye – they described her almost to a tee. The father in particular explained that she tried to seduce him on numerous occasions just to win his trust, pinpointing him as the authority in the household. Was that what Megan had been doing with me? I felt disgusting for ever even fantasising about the two of us. I never betrayed Becca physically, but I'd been with Megan in my head more than once and it was getting too close.

The more I read, the more I was convinced this was the same person. I reached for my phone to make a couple enquiry calls and begin my investigation, but a missed call and a voicemail left me feeling alarmed. Becca always left a text message if she needed anything, so anxiety gripped me a little too tightly as I started to play the message.

The Guest Bedroom

'Jordan, it's me,' my wife said, desperation filling out her frantic voice. 'Things are getting really bad, and I need you to come home. I wanted to leave and... well, I was getting ready to use the car when the tyres were torn open. All of them. It's Megan. She was always the problem and... I've decided I'll tell you everything. Just please come home. We're not safe here right n—'

If this wasn't alarming enough, the next thing I heard before the message ended sent me into a blind panic. It was Megan's voice, only the sweet, charming young woman was gone. In her place was a cruel, horrible, petulant child with nothing but spite in her tone.

'You sneaky little bitch!'

The message ended there. I sat frozen, stunned, my heart rate rapidly increasing. I stared at my computer, the horror story from the report now unfolding in front of me. Suddenly, there wasn't a doubt in my mind that Megan was there with a sinister motive. That's why I ran for the door without so much as grabbing my jacket.

Taking too long could cost me everything.

. . .

The drive home has never felt so long. What usually takes around fifteen minutes is starting to drag. I'm not even fully focused on the road, because I keep dialling Becca's number only to find that it goes straight to voicemail. Her phone is off, out of signal, or – if my dangerously wandering mind is right – broken.

I keep replaying my wife's words in my head. I've never heard her talk like that before. She sounded so hopeless, every word feeling so final. It was as if she knew the end was coming somehow, which only makes my mouth go dry with nervousness. I try to stay focused on the road, leaning into the more logical and practical side of myself that tells me I can't do anything until I finally get to my house.

But I don't even get that far.

I drive past her before it even registers. It's one of those things that's so insanely hard to believe that I'm not even sure I do until it's too late. I pull the car over on the side of the road, then roll down my window and lean out. My eyes aren't what they used to be, but I can clearly see Megan in that familiar jacket, her short, black hair waving in the soft breeze with her back turned. And although I can't see it from here, it's impossible to deny what I saw when I passed.

Jax is in her arms.

I kill the engine and rush out of the car, half-walking, half-running to catch up to her while I try Becca's phone one more time. My imagination is going crazy trying to figure out what's happened, and the part of my brain responsible for denying painful facts ignites. Given who Megan is and the things I believe she's done, I wouldn't put it past her to hurt my wife.

My attention is torn between Becca and Jax, but I know who needs me the most. I pull up my phone, my battery low, desperate not to lose Megan while I dial for emergency services. I've seen this in films a thousand times – the pursuer doesn't call the police until it's too late, when all it would have taken was a simple call. I make that call now, protecting myself.

Protecting Jax.

Megan stops ahead of me. I stop, too. She turns around, and I make no effort to hide. I'm too busy reporting what I see to the voice on the other end, while that crazy woman's eyes fix on me as if I've done something wrong – as if I'm the person walking away with someone else's baby. There's an unspoken language between us as the operator speaks in my ear, telling me to hold the line and that everything is going to be okay. I don't believe her.

Because Megan tightens her grip on my son.

Then turns and runs.

Chapter 26
Becca

JORDAN's superior calms me down with a cup of water. At least that's what he thinks he's done – all that's really happened is he's found a way to shut me up while my anxiety-ridden hands wobble the styrofoam every which way but loose. I'm perched on the edge of a plastic chair in reception, the eyes of every other visitor on me while I keep my head down and pray properly for the first time in my life.

This is a foreign concept to me. I don't really know what I'm doing, what to ask for, or whether I'm supposed to offer something in return. All I know is that I'll never forgive myself if I don't get Jax back safely in my arms. What would Jordan do if I've cost him a son? Even if Jax turns out to be just fine, wouldn't he still be livid about what happened?

After all, there's still the matter of my secret...

The man comes back and sits beside me, his uniform neat and pressed. He tells me his role is chief superintendent, but that means nothing to me. Police ranks always confused me and, although I always tried to take an interest in my husband's work, all the information never really stuck. At the end of the day, all that mattered was that Jordan was happy.

Which he was, until Megan came along.

'We're doing everything we can,' the man tells me, and I'm struggling to recall if he said his name was Greg or Craig. Greg will suffice for now, because there's only so much room in my head at the moment. 'I've put everyone on full alert to let me know if Jordan or your son turn up. And this friend of yours...?'

'Megan,' I say, then think, *but she's not my friend. Far from it.* 'Megan List.'

'Right. We've contacted the authorities closer to her home. With any luck, she'll head back there and be found almost immediately. I know it's hard to believe right now, but we're going to get your little boy back.'

The Guest Bedroom

Obviously, I want to believe him. I just can't. It's like being told I'm going to win the lottery. It's a nice dream, and maybe my entire life depends on it, but will it really happen? Even if it does... what will happen to me? I know Megan almost as much as I know myself, and there's not a chance in hell she'll ever go down without a fight.

Basically, life will never be the same.

Greg sits there with me for a while longer. There's nothing for either of us to say, but I appreciate the comfort while I go out of my mind. I feel awful, probably look just as bad, and most of all I feel helpless. For the first time since Jax was born, I have no idea where he is and I can't do a single thing to help him. What kind of mother does that make me?

I'm trying not to think like that, and thankfully there's no longer time. A uniformed officer pipes up from behind the desk, waving Greg over. Greg pats me on the leg and tells me he'll be right back, then makes his way to the desk. I can't hear what they're saying over the bustle of the police station – too many low conversations, fingers dancing along keyboards, and phone calls being taken far too loud. But their body language tells all; the officer keeps looking over at me, his fingers wrung together. Greg keeps checking around him and looking at his watch. He leans towards the snotty receptionist, who starts typing under pressure and then hands him a small, black radio. It seems like they're going somewhere.

I can only imagine where.

'Mrs. Baxter,' Greg says, returning to me.

Naturally, I shoot to my feet. Water spills from the cup and splashes on to my boots, but I couldn't care less. My entire future lies in the balance, and I'll do anything for a chance to do what's right. 'What's happening? Is something wrong?'

'We've found your husband,' he says. Then, clearly sensing the question of 'alive or dead' on my expression, fills in the blanks. 'He's okay, and so is your son. For now.'

'*For now?*'

'Yes, there's a... situation.'

'What kind of situation?'

Just then, three more officers run by, bursting through the door and out on to the street. My heart is racing, my blood running cold as I get the sense this isn't good news. I look Greg in the eye, searching for answers – for comfort and assurance.

'It's best you come with me,' he says. 'I'll explain along the way.'

The Guest Bedroom

. . .

Greg is letting me ride in his car, which should feel like an honour but really just makes me believe the 'situation' is beyond dire. I'm dying to know what's going on, but he refuses to tell me until we're buckled up and speeding our way through Collingwood. I remember when this was a calm, peaceful town. I mean, it still is, but to me it just feels like somewhere I fled to ever so briefly, and now it's time for me to go away. It's unclear if that means to prison or travelling the country to desperately avoid it. I don't care which, as long as Jax is safe.

When we're on the straight road that leads out of town, I'm just about ready to lose my mind. There are marked police cars ahead of us, the sirens blaring and sending the very rare civilian vehicles out of our way. In all the time I've lived here, I've only seen this happen once before. It was when a killer was on the loose.

I can only hope Megan hasn't killed.

'We got a call from your husband,' Greg tells me, focusing on the road. 'Says he found Megan trying to leave town with your little boy held close to her chest.'

Fog clouds over me as I picture Jax just like that other kidnapped baby – hugged so tight that he can't breathe. In my imagination, my son's face is turning blue as he struggles to breathe, and that sick woman just squeezes him tighter and tighter until...

'Is he okay?' I ask in a short breath. 'Did he say if Jax is hurt?'

'I'm afraid we don't know.'

'Do you at least know where he is?'

'Yes, Jordan has Megan trapped, but she's using your son as a bargaining chip.'

'*A bargaining chip?*' I yell, then roll down the window for some air. It's hard to tell if it's stifling inside or if I'm simply on the verge of having a panic attack. All I know is that it's getting harder and harder to breathe. It's weird – we're only getting closer to my family, but I've never felt farther away. 'What exactly is going on?'

'I'll explain properly when I fully understand myself, okay?'

Greg swallows audibly and shakes his head, then checks the rear-view mirror, signals, and changes lanes to take the slip road out of Collingwood. I don't know where we're heading, because this road only leads to countryside, and maybe a

The Guest Bedroom

harbour town if you wanted to go for a couple more hours. Along the way there's nothing but scenic views of fields and trees and...

Oh.

I understand as soon as I see it. Far ahead of us on the winding country road, the police cars have stopped. The sun is starting to set as a backdrop to the chaotic scene, where police officers gather to deal with the situation. But it's not the cars themselves that draw my attention. It's the thing they're surrounding. The location, although not the exact same one, acts as a throwback to the past that Megan and I share. A past I wanted to leave dead and buried. Now it's repeating itself in the worst way possible, which can bring only one thing with it.

Death.

I DON'T REALLY WANT to admit to myself that this is happening. It's the kind of stuff nightmares are made of. I especially don't want my family to have to suffer for a ridiculous, spur-of-the-moment mistake I made over fifteen years ago.

I feel desperate, but regretful and sad as Greg slams the brakes on the car. Two officers rush towards him as we climb out of the vehicle, then begin to update him on the situation. I can't hear what they're saying because it feels like my soul is floating above my body. As well as that, Jordan comes running from the distance. I stare at him in a daze, doing all I can not to burst into tears. It's all I can do not to collapse.

But he keeps running, and he doesn't stop until I'm in his arms, engulfed by love and relief and pity and sorrow. My tear-stained cheek presses against his chest. A hug like this used to make me feel safe, but now it only makes me feel guilty.

'Jax is alive and well,' he tells me, leaning back enough to look me in the eye.

Relief floods through me, although we're not out of the woods yet. It's hard to see exactly what's going on with the violent shine of sunset peeking over the horizon, but the police are gathered around the bridge. The train bridge, to be exact, where the too-thin figure of Megan List stands with her back against the brick wall.

'What's going on?' I ask.

'Megan has our boy.' Jordan bites his knuckles, restraining his own aggressive outburst at the sound of those horrifying words. 'She's backed into a corner and has nowhere to go, but she's

The Guest Bedroom

threatening to... I don't even know how to say this.'

'Jump?'

Jordan nods. 'It's quite a fall. She might not survive it, and Jax definitely wouldn't. The only saving grace is that the track runs over a stretch of water. I don't know if she's figured that out yet, but if we could try to encourage her towards the further end of the bridge. Then there's a chance they could both survive a fall like that.'

I shake my head, swallowing bile. 'You're talking about our son falling into water.'

'I'm just preparing for the worst, is all.'

'Okay, so what's the *best*-case scenario.'

'We're still trying to figure that out. But she wants to speak to you.'

'Yeah, that makes sense.'

I gaze around at the scene, amazed that they even got this close to controlling the situation. The police are red-faced, struggling to hide their stress as they report updates to their superior. Greg is raking his bony fingers through his thin hair, and it's easy to see that even he's clueless. I wouldn't be surprised if he messed this up even worse than I did.

'What's going on, Becca?'

I turn back to Jordan, feeling weightless and ghostly with anxiety. 'What?'

'Who exactly is this woman? Why is she trying to take our son?'

'She has some mental health issues.'

'Exactly, but why *our* son?'

'Because she knows she can get away with it.'

'Why so sure?'

'It's hard to explain.'

Jordan visibly grinds his teeth and shakes his head. It's obvious he's getting frustrated with me and, to be perfectly honest, I don't blame him. All I've done lately is lie to him, and that's after an entire marriage full of keeping this terrible secret. I wasn't lying when I said I'd tell him everything, however. When this is all over, no matter how it ends, he needs to know the whole truth about my relationship to Megan.

Regardless of what happens to me.

'I promise I'll tell you everything, okay? Can we just focus on the problem?'

'You'd better.' Jordan sighs. 'What will you say to her?'

'Absolutely no clue whatsoever.'

'Well, you better think of something. Our little boy is—'

'Baxter!'

We both turn towards the chief superintendent – Greg. The police officers he was talking to have now dispersed, and he's coming towards us with what can only be bad news. I've seen that look before on a thousand stressed-out men, and one thing is for absolute certain.

What he's about to say can't be good.

Chapter 27
Becca

Greg offers me a look of calm assurance, but I'm not buying it. It's too easy to read the stress in his eyes, the way he's squinting with exhaustion at the pressure he's facing. It's Jordan he focuses on, delivering his line with strict matter-of-factness.

'We're going to advance on her, Baxter.'

Jordan's jaw drops in disbelief. 'You're going to *what?*'

'You heard me. If there's even a slight chance she'll hurt that baby then—'

'If you rush for her then she *will* hurt him. And he's not just any baby. He's ours.'

I reach for Jordan's hand. It's warm but does nothing to comfort me. The sweat-slick palm only tells me he's as anxious as I am. I swallow whatever weird taste is in my mouth and then turn to the setting sun just so I'm not forced to look at Greg or the psycho holding my baby. The sky is getting darker now, all light fading on the horizon. It feels like the sun is going down on my life, too. The night is setting in, and it's going to be cold.

'I'm sorry,' Greg says. 'I really am, but can you imagine what the press would say if they knew we stood by and let her do whatever she wanted to your son? There's not even an alternative, at least not one that we can see.'

'She wants to talk to me,' I snap, whizzing around. 'That's an alternative right there.'

'Right, and then what? She's not exactly ready to give up that child.'

'She'll have to. It's not like there's anywhere for her to run.'

'Then she'll jump. Trust me, I've seen things like this before.'

I close my eyes at the words, as if doing so will help me escape the harm they'll cause. It doesn't work. My heart is breaking, my head is aching – though it's unclear if that's from the stress of the situation or the blow I took not so long ago. I just want all of this to be over. The threats, the worry that keeps me up at night. All of it.

'Sir, I implore you to give us a chance,' Jordan says, squeezing my hand. 'If you're so convinced that she's going to jump either way, the least you can do is let Becca try talking her down. This is between them, after all, so shouldn't she have that opportunity?'

Greg sighs and looks around the scene. I hate him for only caring about how the press makes him look. It makes me believe that all the kindness he's shown so far has just been an act. If anything happens to Jax, I'll definitely assign a portion of the blame to him.

'Fine,' he says. 'You've got five minutes, then we're pushing on.'

As he walks away, my entire body shivers. Jordan turns to hug me, his warm arms enveloping me. I hold him in return, feeling like the biggest piece of crap this world has ever seen. He doesn't deserve this – he could be about to lose his son, and it's all because of a few selfish decisions I've been making this past week. I wish I could turn back the clock and just tell Megan to go sit on a nail. I might have ended up in prison, but at least Jax would be okay.

'You've got this,' Jordan says in my ear, his hot breath breezing on my neck.

The Guest Bedroom

'What if I say the wrong thing and upset her?'

'Just choose your words carefully. If anything happens...' He peels away from me and looks me dead in the eye. 'It's because of her own actions, not yours. You got that? I won't let you blame yourself for any of this.'

If only you knew, I think, taking a breath. I look over at Megan, who's holding my son close to her chest. I wonder if he's awake over there, if he's scared or hungry or tired or confused. I can't hear anything over the chaos on site, but the fact my son needs me is killing me. I must go to him, not only to save him but to face the consequences of my actions from all those years ago. This is all my fault. I realise that.

And now I have to set things right.

MEGAN SMILES while I approach her, that menacing grin making her look like some kind of goblin. My breath is lodged in my dry throat, and I pause to look around at the scene behind me. The police are on edge, watching every little motion while getting ready to storm the scene, ruining everything because my baby doesn't mean to them what he means to me. From where I stand, I can just about see Jordan waving a hand to encourage me on.

I take a deep, steadying breath, then continue.

'That's close enough,' Megan says, clutching my son to her chest. He's not making it easy for her, fidgeting while she sways him gently from side to side. Like his mother should be doing. 'Took your precious time getting here, didn't you? How's the head?'

'It hurts like hell. No thanks to you.'

'Well, that's what happens when you wind me up.'

'I didn't do anything wrong.'

'Hmm, not sure the police would see it that way. Did you tell them?'

'About Mez?'

Megan nods.

'No, and I plan to keep it that way. At least until this is taken care of.'

'You say that like you think you'll win.'

'There's nowhere for you to go.' I try to say it with conviction but stumble halfway through when I realise she's in charge here. If she can't escape then there's nothing to keep her from doing something stupid. That's why I try to pivot. 'Why are you doing this?'

The Guest Bedroom

Megan shrugs, almost dropping Jax. 'You know why. I want to be a mum.'

'No. *This*. Making a scene and summoning me to the front of it.'

'Oh, that's because I need something from you.'

'You have my son. What more could you possibly want?'

'I want you to persuade them to leave.' She nods at the police behind me.

'You must be joking.'

'Is that really something you want to test? There's a pretty big drop behind me.'

It's not a secret that Megan has lost her mind, but it's not until now that I see the true mania behind her eyes. This isn't just a quick thing she wanted to take care of – take someone's baby and try again – she's fully determined to get what she wants and will do absolutely anything to get it. That's how she sees it: winning. Like it's one big game.

'Mez was my friend,' I tell her, clearing my throat. 'It wasn't meant to happen.'

'What's that got to do with the price of fish?'

'Just so you know, I never intended to hurt anyone.'

'Trying to clear your conscience?'

'Not really. Simply making it clear that I'm not like you.'

'What's that supposed to mean?'

'It means I'm not out to hurt people. This thing you're doing, taking other people's babies... it's not right. See, I know about what happened before. That baby you killed—'

'Shut up!'

'I'm just saying, it doesn't have to be this way. You need to level out, get a stable job and show you can be a good mother. There are plenty of adoption agencies that look kindly on single women who have their lives together, and I can help you with that. We all can.'

Megan shakes her head, her face scrunching up with disgust. 'You condescending little bitch. Do you really think I don't know what will happen if I put this little boy down? I'll be arrested in seconds, and what do you think will happen then? How long do you think I'll keep your little secret after you send me away in a set of handcuffs?'

'Honestly, I have no idea. But it's better than leaping off a bridge.'

'Funny.'

'I'm not trying to be. Please, Megan, just... please.'

The Guest Bedroom

She stares at me like she's trying to work out if I'm serious. Meanwhile, Jax starts squirming in her arms. She's not even holding him right, and my body keeps jerking reactively every time he starts tipping more to one side than the other. I'm also aware of the time. Greg gave us five minutes. How long has it been now? Two? Maybe three?

Halfway to losing everything, I muse.

'You know what I want,' Megan says after a long pause. 'Tell them to move, or we'll find out if Jax can fly. Turn around, march back to your little policemen, and make sure they back the hell off so I can get out of here.'

'Please don't—'

'I'm not going to ask again.'

The way our eyes meet, you'd think we've been worst enemies since birth. All I ever did was try to get away from her when I discovered she was poison. Now here I am, face to face with a woman who will bring me to my knees and keep me there. She's dead serious – there's no doubt about that – and somehow I have to report this back to Greg without him rushing her.

My luck is running out.

. . .

When I return from my confrontation with Megan, Jordan studies me with desperate concern. He comes away from some deep, irritated conversation with Greg and meets me by his car where we can hear each other. The stress on his exhausted face is only growing. Even as night is setting in, it's impossible not to see.

'What did she say?' he asks.

I tell him everything, which is basically summed up to her wanting to get away with this. My husband listens quietly until I'm done talking, then takes even longer to process it before coming back to me with anything.

'There's no way that's going to happen,' he says.

'No, I know that.' I exhale slowly, doing my best to control my anxiety and not look over at what the police are doing. The clock is ticking, and my nerves are shot to bits. 'What happened over there? It looked like you were arguing with your boss.'

'That's because I was. I told him there's no way I'll let him advance on Megan.'

'What did he say to that?'

'Obviously, he reminded me that he's my superior and that I have absolutely no say in how this

The Guest Bedroom

goes down. However, we're in the fortunate position to have our future dictated by someone who has kids of his own, so I was able to wrangle something out of it.'

I glance at Greg and see that he's stood back to light a cigarette. This is good news, as very few people would start smoking if they didn't intend to finish. That means he's not planning on pushing things forward. Not yet, at least.

'What's going on?' I ask.

'He's going to let me talk to her.'

I feel the colour drain from my face. If those two end up talking...

'Is that really such a good idea?' I ask.

'It's better than what would be happening,' he checks his watch, 'in thirty seconds.'

'There's no other way around this?'

Jordan looks down at me like I'm on trial. Not that I blame him – I haven't exactly been honest with him since this whole thing started. 'Becca, what exactly aren't you telling me? You mentioned on your voicemail that you'll explain it all.'

'Now's not the time.'

'If it's something that could help...'

'It's not. Not exactly.'

'You promise you'd tell me if it's something that could get our son back?'

I nod. Of course, I think about telling him, but it's really not the time or place. Which is to say I want to but probably won't. It would undoubtedly be best to just finally come out with the truth about what happened all that time ago. About why Megan really came to stay with us and how she ended up taking our son. I know how he'd react, and I'd probably deserve that. Along with the jail time that would follow shortly after.

'Okay.' He sighs. 'It's time. Wish me luck.'

'Good luck.'

I stand back and bite my fingernails, my free hand tucked under my armpit. Jordan is halfway to Megan when I realise I'm hunched over. Greg and the other police have their eyes on me, and I wonder if they've figured it out. I'm probably just being paranoid, but still. It certainly does add to the intense nervousness leaving my body in jitters. There's not even anything I can do from now on – just watch Jordan as he talks privately with Megan.

And pray she doesn't tell him my secret.

Chapter 28
Becca

They seem to talk forever. It goes on and on, and the two of them barely move. It looks like the friendliest conversation in the world – I've no idea if Jordan is smiling, and I doubt it, but Megan's face is alive with humour as the police cars' headlights cast a flood of light on her psychotic features. Now she looks unhinged even for her.

The officers are talking around me. I stand there in the night-time wind that's biting at my cheeks with its surprisingly cold touch. Greg is saying something about how they need to get ready, and I dread to think what will happen if Jordan can't talk her down.

My eyes drift down to Jax, still clutched to Megan's chest like a babe to his mother. But *I'm* his mother, and she'll never take that away from me. It then hits me out of nowhere that, since I refuse to let her go with my son, there are only two ways out of this.

Let the police rush her.

Or let her jump.

Either way, I lose Jax. Either way, I'll end up in prison because it's highly unlikely Megan is going to lose this situation without dropping my big secret. It would be the perfect revenge for her – she'll either get what she wants or die trying but, if I know her at all, she'll make certain I suffer for that dumb mistake fifteen or so years ago.

Jordan turns around briefly to look at me, then turns away. He's very articulate with his hand gestures, and Megan sneaks a quick peek at me, too. I wonder what they're saying. Has he managed to calm her down, even if just a little? The infuriated look on her face says no, but I inch closer in hopes of hearing even just a snippet of the conversation.

Am I being discussed?

Does my husband know about me now?

The conversation goes on, and Jax starts to cry. His little screams pierce the air like bullets, and I cringe at each one. Every instinct inside my body tells me to run to him and give him what he needs. My foot even creeps out a little, but Megan holds up the palm of her hand like a policewoman stopping a vehicle in the street.

'Halt!' I imagine her saying.

She rocks Jax back and forth ever so lightly, which calms him a little but he's still crying. Jordan then takes a step towards Megan, and she backs up against the bridge wall. It's only as high as the middle of her back, and it would be so easy to throw herself off it if she follows through on her threat. And my son would go with her, plummeting to the train tracks below.

I wince and shudder, my face scrunching up in disgust. Jordan turns again, then waves me forward. I tilt my head to one side, not understanding, then he shouts over the buzz and grumble coming from the nearby police cars and the chatter of their officers.

'She wants to speak to you again.'

I turn to look at Greg, who weaves his fingers together and rests his palms on his head. I can see his neck straining – he's dying to get this whole thing over with, but Megan is calling the shots. He looks around, makes his decision, then holds up a couple of fingers.

'Two minutes,' he says. 'Two minutes, and that's all you're getting.'

I nod understanding, not gratitude. With my child's life on the line, he should be giving me a thousand minutes. Still, I'll take what I can get, so I do my best to steady my breathing, clutch my own body to keep warm, and ignore the sweat forming on my brow.

This is it, I tell myself with cruel finality.

This is my last chance to save my son.

When I reach them, Jordan takes a small step back and crosses his arms with his head down. He looks like a headteacher being called in to witness the punishment of a student administered by a member of his staff. It lends to the theory that she's told him about my past, and now I'll never get to kiss or hold or be loved by him again. Is it true, I wonder? Has Megan really given up one of the last playing cards she had? If so, all she has left is Jax.

And he's all I want.

'Your hubby and I were just having a nice chat,' Megan says, then peers over the bridge like she's convincing herself to do the unthinkable. 'The way

The Guest Bedroom

he tells it, you've been asking him to keep me away from your little boy. Is that right?'

I look at Jordan again, who hasn't moved, then turn back to Megan.

'That's right,' I say.

'Doesn't that go against what I asked of you?'

'What do you mean?'

'Well, I gave you seven days to think about handing over the baby. That was out of the kindness of my heart. It's not something you deserved or were entitled to – it was an act of generosity. And you repay me by trying to keep this little bundle of joy away from me?'

I don't know what to say, but there's a lump forming in my throat that doesn't want to be swallowed. My legs have gone weak, and I'm very aware that the next words out of my mouth could cost my only son his life. There's also the time pressure from Greg, who's inching forward and waiting for the right moment to strike. I'm starting to think this is unwinnable.

'I'm really sorry,' I say to Megan, trying a different tactic. 'Not just about that, but about everything that happened between us. You know you were always my best friend, and I didn't mean to just desert you back at home. The truth is, I was a little scared. It felt like you were going on and doing your own thing, and I was losing you. Moving here was... I don't know. Maybe it was my way of reclaiming power.'

'Hah. How's that power treating you now?'

'True, I made some mistakes. But look what's happening. You're about to take away a boy just to punish his mother. Jax has everything to live for. Look at his father.' I gesture towards Jordan, still unmoving. 'You'd break his heart if you stole his son.'

'I'm not *stealing* him!' Megan yells.

Alarm thunders through me, and I soften my voice. 'Okay, not stealing, but taking.'

'That doesn't really matter to me.'

'You don't mind breaking a man's heart?'

Megan laughs. 'Tell her, Jordan.'

As if he's a machine that's just been awakened, Jordan looks up and takes one small step forward. Just enough to be within speaking range. 'Megan has offered to step away from the bridge and let me hold Jax, on the condition that she and I leave town together.'

What?!

I can barely believe what I'm hearing. Nothing should surprise me at this point, but that says little for my shock. Megan has dared to invade my life and kidnap my son, but now she wants my husband, too? The love of my life – the man I married because I truly believed we would spend the rest of time together?

'Tell her what you said,' Megan encourages, beaming now.

Jordan shakes his head. 'Maybe we don't need to—'

'Tell her, you coward.'

'Why don't we just—'

'Tell her!'

The space around me goes silent. I feel lighter than air as I spin around to look at Greg. We must be coming up to two minutes now, because the police are starting to fan out around the scene, protecting every angle so Megan will have nowhere to run.

Nowhere except down.

'I told her we should do it,' Jordan confesses to me, breaking my heart in about two seconds. 'This life you and I have created... it's been wonderful, but if it means saving Jax's life then I'll go to the ends of the earth with this woman. I'll be her lover, her carer, and anything else she needs. In exchange, nobody will hurt our baby. *Nobody.*'

Every word from his mouth cuts deeper than the last. Don't get me wrong, I know he's doing this for our son and not for his own personal gain, but that doesn't make it any easier to hear. Jordan is *my* man, and I'm about to lose him forever for the sake of our son. When it finally clicks that the trade-off means no harm will come to Jax, it becomes easier to swallow.

Easier, but not easy.

Jax starts crying again, his little legs kicking against Megan's stomach. I think about rushing her now, but there's no way in hell I could get to her in time. And if I can't do it from this distance, how on earth does Greg expect to succeed? Perhaps he doesn't want to – it's possible he just wants to be seen trying. 'We did our best,' he might say in a later press conference. But we would all know that was a lie.

If he did his best, we'd have unlimited time to iron this out.

The police are advancing now. I want to step forward again to take care of Jax, but Megan shoots me a don't-you-dare glare. Jordan tries, too, but she shakes her head and tells it straight. 'You're not coming anywhere near me until the deal is in place.'

The Guest Bedroom

'What should I do?' he asks.

'Get rid of them.' She points at the advancing police.

'Stop,' he calls at them.

But they don't listen, and everything turns to shit. My hands clasp over my own mouth as I try to keep in a scream. The officers are moving forward, some running and others securing the scene by blocking the gaps between the police cars. I wheel around to look at Megan, whose eyes reflect nothing but pure anger and frustration. She's beaten – she knows it – and so she'll do what anyone would do when backed into a corner.

'This is your last chance,' she yells. 'Stop right now or I'll jump!'

Finally, I weep. My vision turns blurry, like stained glass. Jordan comes towards me, letting me bury my tear-streaked face in his chest. He holds me there for all of a second, then steps away, distracted. I'm too scared to look but I'm too dumb not to, so I follow his line of sight and see the officers still rushing towards Megan. Not far from them, that wicked woman uses one hand to hoist herself on to the wall, then looks me dead in the eye.

'Stop them,' she says. 'Or say goodbye to your son.'

The policemen don't stop. They're committed. Jordan's eyes widen in terror, and he runs forward. I don't blame him for making that mistake, because I do the same and I'm not even in control of my body. It's the desperation that does it.

Jax screams in her arms. The night air is filled with the horror of multiple shrieks; Jordan's, mine, and our baby's. Beads of sweat are shining like crystals under the headlights' glow as we all run towards her. Then, in a moment that seems like the rest of the world no longer exists, she levels her gaze on me. Without an ounce of emotion in her voice, she says one last thing to me with complete resignation.

'All I wanted was to be a mum.'

She throws herself back. My heart almost stops. Screams erupt in high-pitched, painful frequency. It takes a while for me to realise those screams are my own, and by then Megan is gone. Gravity has taken her and our boy – our beautiful, precious baby boy – and they're no longer in sight. I collapse to the ground and continue to scream,

The Guest Bedroom

covering my ears because I don't want to hear the crunch of them hitting the train tracks below. I close my eyes as tight as possible and wish over and over that I could just rewind time and go back to a week ago, where my son was in my arms and life was okay. But in reality it's not okay.

Life will never be the same again.

Chapter 29
Jordan

IN THE SHORT time it takes for Megan to throw herself (and my son) off that bridge, I'm hit by a sudden rush of memories. Not just the good stuff, like our wedding day, Jax's first laugh, and the meaningful giggles we frequently share during breakfast, but also the more recent past. Things like all those times Megan came on to me.

And what she said only minutes ago.

Becca was behind us back then, standing far enough away that Megan could tell me things in confidence. Things like how Becca knew all along that this was going to happen and did nothing to stop it. Nothing at all to protect our only child and, worse yet, she lied about it.

'That look on your face,' Megan said, jerking a

The Guest Bedroom

finger at me. 'That's the look of a man who's realising his wife is nothing but a big, fat liar. I know that look so well because I've used it so many times. Whenever guys tells me they didn't cheat, that's the look I have. Whenever they promise nothing happened between him and the girl he went out with the other night. It's all lies, Jordan, and you must be sick of it just like I was.'

I didn't know what to say. Words had somehow eluded me. I rotated at the waist to look at my wife, who was hunched over like a hedgehog trying to protect itself. Her expression was that of a victim, terrified of what might happen to her and her son. Only then did I begin to question what might happen to them *because* of her.

'How am I supposed to believe you?' I tried, dying to hear any good reason at all.

'Oh, come on. We both know she's been keeping something from you. How else did she explain my sudden appearance here? Not to mention my reluctance to find a job.'

'She... didn't.'

'Then what *did* she tell you?'

'Only that I should keep you two separated.' I nodded at my son.

It was true. That night in bed, Becca had

begged me not to ask any more questions. Now I knew why she wanted that so badly, but how had she known Megan was a threat? The short answer was because she'd had a secret of her own. A pretty bloody big one.

Megan told me this with no remorse whatsoever. I listened to her explanation of an incident that had occurred almost two decades ago. It sounded familiar because I'd read it before, on newspaper clippings that were left on our kitchen counter.

'That young lady was Becca's friend?' I asked, emotional wounding taking its toll.

'Something like that. She killed her, Jordan. I might have delivered the finishing blow, but it was Becca who pushed her in the first place. If I didn't hit her with that rock, Mez would have died regardless, only slower. All I did was help.'

A sudden, foul taste rested on my tongue, like bile. I didn't want it to be true, but it was. My wife was a killer, intentionally or not, and she'd been hiding it from the entire world for all those years. How was I supposed to trust a person like that? Even if she was the mother of my child, how could I sleep at night knowing she could hide something from me for so long?

The Guest Bedroom

'You don't have to stay with her,' Megan said.

'No? It's not like I have another option.'

'Actually... you do.'

'What's that?'

'Come with me.'

I shook my head non-stop as she offered a deal to me. If I went with her and ensured the police stayed off our backs, she wouldn't hurt Jax. Given the circumstances, it seemed like a good idea. My liar of a wife clearly wasn't capable of looking after our kid, so why not? Besides, there were worse-looking women than Megan on this earth.

But there were also more sane people...

No. Becca was my wife. I would love her until the day we died. That was what we'd said in our vows, and I'd meant every word. There was no way I was leaving her, even if this secret got out. We could find a way to cope, but first we needed our son back safely in our arms. There was only one way to make that happen, so I looked Megan in the eye and lied to her.

'Okay,' I said. 'Let's tell Becca that we're leaving.'

. . .

Time catches up to me, anguish rushing into my stomach like a flood. My breath leaves me in an instant, and I scream as my wife does, all hope fleeting. Not a single rational thought crosses my mind when I run towards the bridge wall, slamming into it with great force.

There, far below in the blackest of night, is an unmoving shape. My heart breaks, and painful, acidic misery floods through my body. That's my son down there, I realise with absolute horror, and the bitch who took him from us. I stare, a hollow emptied out inside me as I pray for it to move – for any slight motion to indicate they might be alive. That my son didn't suffer in all of this, and that there's hope yet.

But all that shape does is vanish, swallowed by the night's darkness as the surrounding trees block out the moonlight. Empty, destroyed, I pivot to see Becca crumpled on the floor with the weight of her grief. I feel compelled to go to her, to comfort her, but I don't have the strength required to move. I don't have the—

My baby's scream emanates from the pitch black. Hope springs me to life. I peer over the wall and squint into the darkness, that image below still impossible to spot. But that's definitely my baby's cry I heard. Only it's gone now, and I realise what has happened.

Megan and Jax hit the water.

Which means they're still alive.

For now.

Without a second to lose, I run along the side of the bridge and hit the bushes, speeding through them as the foliage tears at my legs. It doesn't bother me, because all I want to do is get down there and find Jax. Except the sudden silence terrifies me, cold fear bolting through me like lightning as I rush down the grass hill towards the tracks. I gain enough distance – thirty metres, twenty, ten – and hit the water between the rails with a splash, feeling around in the freezing water for my son but feeling nothing other than empty space.

Please, I think, unsure if I'm saying it aloud.

Please let my little boy live.

Chapter 30
Becca

I feel pathetic. I feel awful.

I feel weak.

Who knows how long it's been since I collapsed, covering my eyes and ears while curling up like it would protect me from some kind of explosive blast? For the faintest flicker of a moment, I experience true shame for the coward I've become. But that still doesn't stop me from wanting to stay here forever, where it's safe and nothing from the real world can get in.

Nothing except that sound.

Women have spent millennia growing accustomed to it. Biologists believe the human ear has become so finely tuned to respond to it that mothers can hear it from a mile off. Some say we can sense it even when our ears themselves don't pick up the sound, kind of like how twins can feel each other when something goes horribly wrong.

Something *has* gone horribly wrong.

But that sound is real.

Daring to convince myself that I can really hear it, I raise my head to investigate. Jordan is by the side of the bridge, hurling himself through a thick bush that seems to engulf him. Though it doesn't seem to hinder his speed – he's moving like a racing car, tearing through the thicket like his life depends on it. Like our son's life depends on it.

'Jax?' I say weakly, my voice little more than a nervous croak.

I strain to listen, and that's what I hear. Jax is crying. No, *screaming*. Some of the police officers are gathered around the bridge, pointing at whatever is lying on the tracks. The others are following Jordan, but they're trailing behind and struggling to keep up.

It takes everything I've got to clamber to my feet, pushing myself up from the hard tarmac road. Greg rushes to my side, his hands reaching out to help, but I push him away. There's a dark place in my heart, reserved for my hatred of him and the foul, lasting memory of how he risked my son's life for the sake of good press. Not that I'm entirely innocent, but I can hardly think straight through all this trauma.

On my feet at last, I run to the bridge. Just as I arrive, my knees smacking into the brick, I hear a thick splash from far below. My eyes take forever adjusting to the darkness but, when they do, it's easier to make out what's happening down there. As soon as I see it, I suddenly know how the women feel in those superhero films once they've been saved. A breath of relief blows through my lips, but my body still stiffens with tension.

Jordan has dived into the water between the rails. Far along the track, a small bead of light illuminates like a tiny moon. A long horn blares, and then a hiss rockets through the metal. I scream at the top of my lungs while Jordan splashes around down there. He's under thirty seconds from a grim fate that I'll never recover from.

Which means Jax is in danger, too.

I feel helpless, watching from high above while the officers yell at Jordan. One of them dares to rush on, leaping over the track and reaching into the water for my husband's hand. He finds purchase and pulls, then I see Jax – God, he actually has Jax in his arms! – as he's hauled out of the water and on to the wooden planks between the rails. Meanwhile, the train grows nearer. Its engine sounds like a monster. It rips through the dark as its beam grows brighter. I clutch brick, sharp edges bleeding my palms.

'Get off the track!' I scream so loud it actually hurts.

But my voice is shrunk in the blast of a rushing train. It's too dark to see what happened. I just watch, still helpless as each carriage passes under me. The bridge shakes with the sheer force, and I try not to think that my family has been hit by it. The very concept makes me sick, and it takes forever for the train to finally pass on.

Then it becomes clear.

Jordan and the officer made it out of harm's way. I shriek with relief and excitement, moving along the bridge to get a better look. I'm grinning from ear to ear, hardly able to believe my luck as I find my husband and son safe and sound.

And I shouldn't believe it.

Something is wrong down there. Jordan lets out a guttural roar of devastation as he and the officer gather around Jax. I can't see what they're looking at or what the problem is, but there's an awful, unsettling feeling in the pit of my stomach that burns like fire. All I can think of is that something terrible has happened.

And it's happened to Jax.

There's no sign of Megan as I throw myself down the hill towards them. The officers behind me have found their torches and are aiming their beams at the scene below as we all make our way down. I almost trip and tumble a hundred times, but I don't care. If anything, it would just reunite me with them quicker and allow me to see what's gone wrong.

When I reach the bottom, I stop dead in my tracks. My chest heaves up and down as I catch my breath, looking over at my own personal hell. Jax is lying on the ground, his eyes closed as he faces the sky. Jordan snaps at the officer to step back and then begins to perform CPR, pushing on our baby son's chest and then administering air to his lips.

There's something poetic about the silence that follows. It's hard to describe exactly, but it's as if the world has stopped turning. My stomach hasn't,

The Guest Bedroom

however, and is knotted into all sorts of excruciating shapes while I hold my breath and pray.

There's no luck.

I step forward, but only a little. I don't want to crowd them or throw Jordan off his game. He's in the zone and, just like I've always trusted him, I know that he's the perfect man for the job. Jax's life hangs in the balance and I know that if anyone can perform a miracle, it's my husband. The man of my dreams, who almost ran off with—

The last thing I should be thinking of is Megan, but I can't help it. My eyes roam around the dark scene beside the track, and nobody has even made a slight mention of the woman who threw my son off a bridge. Maybe she drowned in the water, or maybe the train hit her. Either one of them would be acceptable to me, as dark as that sounds. It *does* sound like something a murderer would say, and isn't that what I am?

As I watch, Jordan begins to press Jax's chest again. The more time goes on, the harder it is to believe he can be resuscitated. It goes a long way to putting things in perspective and, knowing he could die at any minute, I only hope more that something has happened to Megan. I dread to think what might happen in the future if she made it out of here alive. Especially without taking my baby boy away. I imagine she'll feel scorned.

The best sound in the world comes out of the dark. Jax sputters. There's a short, splashing sound, like a fountain coming to life with a weak little spurt. There's a deep, raspy cough, followed by a cry I never knew I'd want to hear so much. Jordan scoops him into his arms, and time unfreezes. Tears rain down my cheeks. The officers cheer. I run forward and throw my arms around the two of them, planting kiss after kiss on Jax's cheeks, eternally grateful for him to be alive. I don't know if anything is broken or bruised, but the distant wail of an ambulance's sirens will see to that. For now, I can just breathe knowing that the danger has passed – finally, it's *passed* – and my son is alive and in our arms again.

Finally, everything will be okay.

THERE IS one thing left undone, and nobody speaks of it.

I know the officers are down there looking for her and, as we sit on the back step of an ambulance and the police continue clearing things up around us, I'm too afraid to ask. As time goes on, it's

The Guest Bedroom

looking less and less likely that Megan will be found.

'Stop worrying,' Jordan says as he hands Jax over to me. The blanket he's wrapped in starts to come undone, but Jordan tightens it. 'It might not seem like it, but we got our son back and we're still in one piece. This is one hundred per cent a win.'

'I know. It's just that you were going to... You know.'

'Run away with Megan?'

I nod.

'No, that was just me trying to get our son back.'

Believing him fully, I half-smile and hold our little boy close to me. Jax fits nicely on my chest, and I feel his warmth as his sleepy little head turns three or four times to find a comfortable position. It's been a little while since his last feed, but there's nothing we can do about it. If he gets desperate then we'll try a one-off breastfeed to get us home. Until then, I pat his bottom and let him sleep. I can't stop sniffing his head, over the moon that we have him back safely after all of this.

I've also had my head dressed by a paramedic. They've cleaned up the cut (I didn't even realise there was a cut until they'd said) and told me it will leave a nasty mark for at least a couple of weeks. Honestly, that's the least of my concerns.

I just want Megan brought to justice.

On the other hand, though... do I? It's pretty much guaranteed she'll view herself as the victim in all of this, and there's not a doubt in my mind she'll be out to punish me. That might mean a little more than turning up on our doorstep for a second time – maybe with the intention of hurting someone – but there's also the matter of a certain little secret.

I look up at Jordan, and he looks away. I wonder if he knows. There's no way to ask him without giving it all away, but I open my mouth to try anyway. Nothing comes out, but Jordan senses there's something on my mind. He shakes his head and looks away.

'We'll talk about it at a better time,' he says.

Panic ignites within me. He knows – he must do – but then why isn't he saying something? Perhaps this is him being a man, taking care of his family and not getting hung up on the details. That won't last forever, so I cherish this calm before the storm.

A few minutes of silence later, Greg finds his way over to us. Jordan screws his face up in absolute disgust, and it's taking all my strength not to stand up and slap him for what he did. He knows how we feel – his lack of eye contact says it all – but he doesn't address it.

'Our men have searched high and low, but there's no sign of this Megan woman whatsoever.' Greg scratches his head, almost like a cartoon of a frustrated man. 'We'll keep the search running and share this with surrounding towns. Do you have a picture of her?'

'Not a recent one,' I say, Jax starting to stir in my arms, 'but I probably have something.'

'Good. Have Jordan send everything to me, will you?'

I nod, and Jordan turns his back on his own superior. As Greg leaves, I wonder how uncomfortable things are going to be at work from now on. Jordan has never handled confrontation too well. That is to say he does what needs to be done but once confessed to me it makes him feel awkward. I wouldn't be surprised, however, if his anger trumps his discomfort this time. After all, his son nearly died due to Greg's mistake.

But we can't get hung up on that right now. Personally, I'm just grateful we're all back together as a family again. Tonight could have gone a whole lot worse and, although it sounds sickeningly optimistic, I have a feeling everything is going to be okay.

At least, that's what I hope.

Megan *is* still out there.

Chapter 31
Becca

Week by week, our little family returns to normal. Our new version of normal anyway. It's not exactly a healthy approach to treating trauma, but we seem to be completely ignoring the fact Megan is still on the run. It does make me wonder if she died in the fall, but that's ridiculous – if she was hit by that train, we would know about it. I actually know someone who saw a man get hit by a speeding train once and, apparently, there were limbs everywhere. Not the prettiest sight to imagine, but it goes a long way to make me believe she's still alive.

I'm keeping an eye over my shoulder at all times, of course. Jordan has taken a little time off work, and he's spending every waking minute with Jax and me. It's actually become a little awkward, because I'm watching his every move and dying to know just how much Megan told him. Is he keeping his thoughts to himself, or is he utterly oblivious to the truth?

Time will tell... I hope.

We do have a little security in the press who keep hounding us. It sounds backwards, but let me explain. See, I've never slept this badly in my life. Every night is full of startling wake-ups to check the house after terrifying dreams about Megan breaking in to kill us all. I'm constantly on edge, but there's a knock on our door at least three times per day from someone wanting to interview us or strike a book deal. One person even proposed a documentary for one of the streaming services, but the last thing I need is people looking into my past.

They certainly won't like what they find.

But the way I see it, we're safe for as long as all that attention is on us. The police send people over to watch the house here or there, but it's happening with less frequency than before. With every passing week they seem to drop a few hours here or there, then a day, and before we know it they've

The Guest Bedroom

gone completely. Sadly, even the journalists start to lose interest, and then we're finally alone like we used to be.

Well, not *exactly* like we used to be.

Jax has started walking (albeit badly), which is wonderful and frightening all at once. Time is going far too fast, which makes me think he'll be climbing soon. I start to think of the future, picturing myself dropping him off at school or him hanging out at the park with his friends. It would be all too easy for Megan to swoop in and take him, or perhaps even hurt him.

That's when I'm struck by the grim realisation that this is going to go on forever. At least unless Megan is found, dead or alive, I'll be watching my son's every move until the end of time, eagle-eyed and ready to go for the jugular of anyone who dares try to take him.

All I have to do is wait.

The real surprise is that my mother has suddenly taken an interest.

I was minding my own business this morning when she arrived at our front door. Naturally, I reeled back, because although she's had our address since the dawn of time, she hasn't once paid a single visit to our home. I wasn't prepared at the time and, although I appreciated her making the effort, I told her to come back later so I could have a chance to tidy up and get Jax fed while Jordan is back at the police station negotiating his return to work. The way I see it, if she's that interested then she'll come back no problem.

Just as I've managed to put Jax down for his nap, there's a knock on the door. Jax stirs, so I grab the baby monitor and sneak downstairs, closing the door behind me. There isn't a force in this world that could make me leave him where I don't have a constant view, so I keep it in my hand as I let my mother inside and give her a tour of downstairs.

'It's lovely,' she says with a very slight tone of pride. 'You've done very well.'

'Thank you,' I tell her, hiding my smile.

But it's really not my doing. My half of the inheritance covered some of the house, whereas Jordan's inheritance and his salary take care of the rest. At this point I'm just a stay-at-home mum. Well, not *just* that. It's actually a lot of hard work, and the only spare time I get is while Jax naps.

The Guest Bedroom

Which I usually fill by cleaning the house or, in this case, reuniting with family.

'Why are you here?' I ask bluntly, leading her into the kitchen where I boil the kettle and drop two teabags into mugs. 'No offence – I'm glad you're here – but there has to be a reason you're showing up out of the blue.'

My mother smiles thinly and stares at her polished boots. 'I've been hearing a lot about you on the news lately. I wanted to make sure you're okay.'

'I'm fine. That can't be the only reason?'

'No, there's... all this talk about almost losing you and the baby made me think. If something happened to you, I wouldn't have a single thing left in this world to live for. Now, I know we never really saw eye to eye, but maybe this is an opportunity to start fresh.'

I take a deep breath as the kettle water begins to bubble. Keeping the baby monitor in sight, I fold my arms across my chest and stare at her. This is dangerous because if I get too attached and she just turns out to be the same old mother she always was, I'm exposing myself to a potential lot of misery. Over the years, I've made my peace with being mostly motherless. Dangling this carrot in front of me is fine, but only if I actually get to taste it.

'That sounds nice,' I tell her, noticing the first genuine smile she's ever given. 'But let me be honest, I don't need a mum any more. I'm almost thirty-six. What I need right now is a friend, and Jax needs a grandmother. Is that something that appeals to you?'

'More than you'll ever know.'

'And your recent affinity for alcohol?'

'Already gone. Promise.'

I try to believe her, and I'm actually starting to. Over the next few days, she drops by every single morning to spend time with Jax. I never let her out of my sight, of course, due to my extreme paranoia that this has something to do with Megan. It's ridiculous – it really is – but a mother needs to be careful. Especially one who's gone through what I have.

A relationship is forming, however, and it's lovely to see. Jax is really starting to adore his grandmother, and I love seeing them together. She's been given a second chance to care for a child, and this time it's really paying off. Maybe she's right – maybe this whole situation really has sparked something maternal inside her. If she had

The Guest Bedroom

always acted like this, years ago with me, she could have been a really good mum.

That's when I start to imagine it.

Jax is in her arms, being fed and played with. He'll have help with his homework in years to come. She's proving herself to be a responsible adult with some actual human emotions for once. It warms my heart to watch them together, but I'm alarmed by the thought this stirs within me. What if she had to take over? What if I end up in prison for manslaughter, and Jordan isn't able to take care of our son by himself?

It gets me thinking. I'm done with the awkwardness of not knowing how much Megan told him. The painful silences around him are driving me insane, and there's nothing I want more than to be done with this extreme discomfort.

So I make up my mind. When Jordan comes home, I'll sit him down.

Then, like it or not, I'll tell him everything.

Telling your husband you're a killer is never an easy thing. Not that I know just yet – I've been keeping this a secret for far too long. His devotion to our family, his unwavering trust and attention, only makes me feel more guilty about it. Is this how a good man should be rewarded? By lying to him constantly about the person his wife really is?

My mother left around four. I've spent three hours getting Jax fed, played with, read to, and put to bed early just so I can have a spare minute to think about how best to approach it. This isn't something I've done before, and I have no idea how it's going to play out. Hopefully, he won't leave me for it, but let's not kid ourselves.

Jordan is a policeman.

The car grumbles its way up the drive, crunching the gravel beneath its weight. The engine dies, the door slams, and my anxiety is sky-high. When he comes in the door and smells the food in the kitchen, he gravitates that way with a big smile on his face.

It kills me that I have to take that smile away.

'We need to talk.'

The words come out of my mouth with depressing seriousness. Jordan knows what this means. He nods as if he's known it this whole time and he's been holding it in for as long as possible. Then he blows out a long, exasperated breath and comes to join me in the living room. Rather than sitting beside me and letting me lay on him like he often does, he takes a seat in the armchair across from the sofa I'm sitting on, one hand tucked into his armpit and the other wrapped around his mouth. I know a nervous man when I see one, and this is it.

'I think it's time we discussed those newspaper clippings you found on the counter,' I say in a ragged breath, on the verge of crying. 'There's more to that story than I led you to believe. They don't belong to Megan at all...'

'Oh?'

'They belong to me.'

It's shocking how easily the rest falls out of my mouth. This is the result of a long, healthy marriage to a good man. Jordan listens blank-faced as I spill my guts on the big, terrible thing I did to Mez. I tell him about Megan's reaction to it all, then the years that came after. I tell him why I had to hide it from him, and what Megan threatened me with when she first came into this house. Then, as if it will change anything at all, I fight back the tears and apologise sincerely for all the bad that happened because of me. Not Megan – *me*.

Then the most amazing thing happens. Jordan finally moves after not showing a single emotion all this time. He pushes himself up from the armchair and comes over to me, dropping to his knees. He takes my hands in his, kisses me on the cheek softly, then whispers in my ear something I never thought would leave his lips.

'I know.'

My blood runs cold. I seize up, unsure if I heard him correctly. Then Jordan sits back on his heels and looks me dead in the eye once again. I half-expect him to grill me – to tell me that this is how our family is going to come to an abrupt, screeching halt.

But he doesn't.

'Megan told me,' he says.

My jaw drops. 'You've known this whole time?'

'Since the incident on the bridge.'

'And you haven't said a thing.'

'I didn't have to. You're my wife. You made a mistake, and it was long before we met. Do I wish you hadn't lied to me all this time? Of course, but I understand why you did it.' Jordan squeezes my hand and smiles. 'This is between us, okay? You're not going to be arrested, but let me just say that ignorance is bliss. If we're going to carry on then I don't ever want to hear about it again. Is that fair enough?'

I finally cry, nodding rapidly as my chin falls

on to his shoulder. I release a long, painful weep, holding him close because this isn't the end at all. There's one more thing I need from him, but I don't have the faintest clue how to ask. I'll just have to keep it to myself.

For now.

Chapter 32
Becca

It was a fair request, but that didn't make it any easier.

Over time, it felt like Jordan and I were becoming more and more distant. There was this gaping chasm between us, the kind of void that could only be filled by a long, detailed discussion about everything that had happened in the years leading up to this moment.

I'm actually pretty angry at myself. I was so preoccupied by telling him all the facts, I didn't stop long enough to realise that how I felt was equally important. For instance, he now knows I pushed Mez down that bank, but he doesn't know how it felt to see that look of shock in her eyes. He knows I avoided Megan for years because I was

The Guest Bedroom

scared of her, but he has no idea about the number of sleepless nights and horrific dreams I endured. That disastrous event shaped me into the woman I am today – better or worse, but mostly worse – and he doesn't seem even remotely interested in how that came to be. There's a phrase I'm tempted to assign to this – words he used – but it tastes too harsh on my tongue to use it.

'Ignorance is bliss.'

That was really what I was seeing: ignorance for me, bliss for him. Hot, sunny days felt cold and gloomy to me. I wanted to talk, to let every emotion come pouring out of me. Isn't that the point of a marriage? Having someone there to hold your hand and talk you through your every thought and feeling? It's a sort of mutual trust, but I do understand.

I took advantage of his trust.

Anyway, I knew what the deal was. 'Don't talk about it.' I've been doing a pretty good job of it until just now, when an urgent feeling of expression overwhelms me. Jordan is just minding his own business, reading his latest novel with Jax asleep on his chest, when I suddenly look up from my phone and blurt it out.

'We need to talk about what happened?'

Without so much as looking at me, Jordan sighs

heavily, leans his head back on the sofa, and closes his eyes. 'I knew this day was coming. I just didn't realise it would be so soon.'

'What's that supposed to mean?'

'You promised to let this go.'

'True, and I'm sorry, but we need to communicate.'

'Can't you just tell it to a therapist?'

'And get locked up?' I put my phone down and sit up straight, patting his leg to let him know this isn't an attack. It's merely something that needs to come off my chest. 'Can we please talk about it just this one time? All I need is to get it off my chest.'

Jordan opens his eyes, gazing up at the beautiful oak beams of our ceiling. 'Why?'

'Because it's eating me up inside.'

'Please don't forget I'm a policeman.'

'Oh, you're going to arrest me?'

'No, but... Listen. I can do anything in the world to help you process this, but it's vital that we don't have this conversation again. I'm here for you as a husband, lover, and friend. I'd do anything for you – I'd *kill* for you – but don't want to be questioned about it after.'

I shake my head and lower it. 'Nobody's asking you to kill.'

The Guest Bedroom

'Just tell me what to do. Other than talk it out.'

'Well, there is one thing...'

'Anything. You name it, we'll do it.'

So I tell him, and we pack the car as soon as Jax wakes up.

THE CEMETERY IS GREENER than any park. It has perfectly clipped hedges all the way along each side. The gravel path stripes through the middle, like a river dividing two beautifully green banks resplendent with manicured grass. Even the headstones are in excellent condition, nicely polished and some probably refurbished. This is where the rich people bury their dead, and the only rich person I know is residing right at the back, in a small lot surrounded by tall trees.

Jordan is at my side, his sweat-coated hand holding mine. It's a little gross, but I don't mind. It just feels right having him here, supporting me exactly like he promised he would. The thing is, I don't need him right now. Before, yes, and definitely after, but this is something I have to do all by myself if I'm to truly get my thoughts out.

'Could I go alone?' I ask.

'I'll be right here.'

Jordan kisses me on the cheek, his stubble grazing my skin. As he stands back to admire the clear blue sky, I take in the sight of him for just a moment. It's weird not having Jax in our arms for the first time since the Megan affair, but my mother has that taken care of for the rest of the day. With a constant video feed, no less. Not that I don't trust her, but... well, I don't.

I turn on my heel and walk the remainder of the long path until I reach the gravestone. It's a secluded marker, the stone showing signs of moss that the keeper hasn't fully managed to clear off. My heart bleeds as I drop to my knees and wipe the time-worn granite. It's stubborn, requiring my fingernails to scrape it off. A disturbing thought enters my mind then.

The last time Mez saw this hand, it was killing her.

I shake my head and cry instantly, feeling utterly disgusted with myself. I have no right to be feeling sorry for myself after taking this poor young woman's life. It wasn't even just her life I took – she was deprived of all her hopes and dreams, her family kept from the closure they deserved. I can't help thinking of Megan and how she insisted we buried the body. She was never even found and laid to rest at this grave. The headstone marks nothing at all.

'Words can't describe,' I croak, then cover my mouth with a hand as warm tears seep on to my cheeks. I say the rest through my fingers, barely able to believe this is happening. Did I really believe this would be enough to help me move on?

'The things we did to you. Megan and I, we... I want you to know that this was never meant to happen. When I pushed you, it was only to keep you out of harm's way. If I knew you would fall like that, I'd have let you take the hit. If I knew Megan would pick up that rock...'

My nose runs, and I'm a blubbering mess. Thankfully, Jordan was kind enough to hand me a pack of tissues as we left the car, and now I finger through them and pull out a small handful of sheets just to mop up my disgusting face. As I do this, I glance over at Jordan, who has his back turned to give us the privacy we need.

I return to Mez or, as the grave states, Mary-Ann.

'There's no making up for this, that's an absolute fact, but please know that if Megan ever shows up then I won't let this keep me from shouting the truth. I'm going to send your parents a letter and tell them what happened, okay? It's not much, but at least they'll know for sure. I'll keep names out of it for now, but if I ever need to tell them... you can count on me.'

That's the best I can do before hugging the grave, pouring out my heart in the form of countless apologies. Mez and I were never close, but we could have been. It reminds me that we could have ended up in college together, and that's another thing I took from her with that push. Accident or no accident, that beautiful person was killed by me and—

No. I won't say her name. The thought alone stands in the way of our closure. I know it's weird, but I kiss the stone and say goodbye to Mez once and for all. She deserved so much better than this, and she had an amazing life to lead. It's only right that she at least gets the apology, and I hope that maybe up in Heaven she can hear what I have to say.

Walking away is the hardest part, but it has to be done. I turn my back on her and wipe away the remaining tears, ready to start the rest of my life. It doesn't feel good to keep this secret to ourselves, but if it's what we have to do in order to survive, then we will.

The Guest Bedroom

'Are you okay?' Jordan asks.

'Hard to say, but maybe.'

'Whatever it takes to put it behind us.'

'Yes, behind us.' I go silent as those words fall on quiet, open air, not at all liking how they sound. It seems so dismissive, as if a singular act can allow us to live the rest of our lives guilt-free. I'm reminded of that awful phrase again: ignorance is bliss.

'Are you ready to go?' Jordan asks, putting his arm around me.

I nod and walk with him back to the car. Later on, I have a letter to write before sneakily finding a way to deliver it to Mez's parents. I can only imagine how torn up they'll feel to receive it and know for certain what happened, but over time they might get a chance to move on. Just like Jordan and I intend to as we head back home. Not that we'll get that far yet.

Because I have something else to say.

'WHATEVER IT TAKES to put it behind us,' was what he said.

It didn't feel right when he said it, but I keep my thoughts to myself until we're back in the car.

We're silent for too long, and Jordan doesn't even put the key in the ignition. Perhaps he's sensed that I'm on to him, and now it's like he's waiting to have this over and done with.

'There's more to it, isn't there?' I ask.

Jordan nods, then looks down at his keys. He's trying to think of how to phrase it, and I don't want to rush him. After the patience and kindness he's shown me, it's the least he deserves. So I just sit there in the painful, growing silence until he speaks.

'Megan is dead,' he says.

It doesn't hit me that hard. Somehow, I always knew. The way he was always so relaxed about it, promising she'll never come back and hurt us. That calm reassurance was too genuine to be ignored, but it never really registered until today. Now that it's out in the open...

'You don't take a man's son and live to regret it.'

'No, you don't.'

'She had to die.'

'Yes,' I say. 'How did it happen?'

'I went looking for her the next day.' He rubs his eyes with the heels of his hands. 'Didn't have to look very far. She was hiding in the woods around that bridge. The police ran right by her in the dark,

The Guest Bedroom

and she stayed there overnight. Too scared to move, she said.'

'What happened when you found her?'

'I gave her my fishing knife and a little persuasion.'

'She killed herself?'

Jordan nods.

'And the body?'

'Left for the wildlife.'

The irony is astounding. Just like she'd left Mez to be eaten and rot out in the open, Megan was now sharing the same fate. Is it weird that I feel a cold stab of misery over this? Maybe I'm too kind a person, but I never wanted anyone to die. It should also change the way I feel about my husband, but it doesn't. Like he said, he'd kill for me.

'Now we have each other's secrets,' he says. 'Which is why I really don't want to talk about it. So can we please just go home and start our lives all over again? Please, this is the last thing I ever want to rest on my conscience and—'

'Do you need closure?'

'What?'

I lean over the seat and cup his face in my hands. 'You came all this way to give me closure.

I'm just letting you know that if there's anything you can do to ease the pain inside yourself, I'll be right here to do it with you. You can even do it yourself if you prefer, but it's not a one-way street. I'm here for you, just like you're here for me.'

It's not the perfect relationship any more, but it's definitely a strong bond. Jordan half-smiles and kisses me, then slides the key into the ignition and brings the car to life. I sit back and put on my seat belt, then enjoy the silence while we drive back to our home in Collingwood to start from scratch. Only this time, I know we're safe, because Megan is gone.

And my big secret died with her.

Epilogue – Jordan

I told Becca I was working today.

I lied.

It's been a whole day since we got back from the cemetery. That was hard work for sure, but we got through it together. Just like we'll get through anything together. But what's imperative to our survival as a family is that there's nothing to worry about – no looking over our shoulders for the rest of our lives and wondering if our secrets are safe.

'Whatever it takes.'

I climb down the ladder and into the dark that smells foul and stale with decades of nature's abuse. It's cold down here, and the water is flooded up to my ankles. As far as I'm aware, nobody in Collingwood has the faintest clue this under-

Epilogue – Jordan

ground war bunker exists. Even I didn't know about it until I went out looking for Megan.

And I found her.

'Tell me you brought me more food,' she says.

'No, I didn't.'

I hear splashing but don't see her. It's too dark.

'Because you've come to let me out?' she asks.

'No.'

A pause. 'Then why?'

'You're not going to need it.'

'Explain.'

Talking her through my evil plan isn't exactly something I want to do, but it will help clear my conscience in the years to come. I wade through the water to the back of the room, using the light on my phone to illuminate the bunker. Megan is in the corner, her hands still cuffed to the iron rail on the far wall. Her hair is wet and tangled, her clothes drenched. She looks a mess. Certainly not someone I would sleep with. It's amazing how far we've come.

'The only reason you're alive is because I couldn't work out what to do with you,' I tell her solemnly. 'I can't trust you enough to let you go, and that's if I even wanted to. Let me make it clear:

Epilogue – Jordan

I don't. You tried to kill my son, and you're going to burn in hell for that.'

'I'm so sorr—'

'Save it.' I take a step closer just to get one last look at her, then deliver the finishing blow – the final line that's bound to make her scream her head off. 'I'm not a killer either, so it's not like I can directly do that. What I *can* do is leave you here to rot, just like you left that poor young woman all those years ago. Trust me, it's the least you deserve.'

'Jordan? Wait, I—'

'Goodbye, Megan.'

It actually pains me to do it, but I somehow manage to turn my back on her. She screams a high-pitched, monster-like wail that she can hardly be blamed for. As I head towards the ladder and start to climb, she becomes more shrill and desperate. She changes tactics on the fly, alternating between threatening to kill me and begging forgiveness.

But we're way past forgiveness.

The concrete slab slides across the hole, sealing her inside. Who knows how long it will take for her to starve to death? I don't really care, to be honest. As long as nobody finds her out here – which is highly unlikely – Becca and I can go back to living

Epilogue – Jordan

our happy lives and finally put all of this behind us. I carry that thought with me back to the road, where I climb into my car and drive away without taking so much as a single glance behind me.

It's time to continue living again, I tell myself.

Whatever it takes.

For other books by AJ Carter, visit:

www.ajcarterbooks.com/books

About the Author

AJ Carter is a psychological thriller author from Bristol, England. His first book, *The Family Secret*, is praised by critics around the world, and he continues to regularly deliver suspenseful novels you can't put down.

Sign up to his mailing list today and be the first to hear about upcoming releases and hot new deals for existing books. You'll also receive a FREE digital copy of *The Couple Downstairs* – an unputdownable domestic thriller you won't find anywhere else in the world.

www.ajcarterbooks.com/subscribe

Printed in Great Britain
by Amazon